A PLATE OF RED HERRINGS

Mysteries by Richard Lockridge

A PLATE OF RED HERRINGS
MURDER IN FALSE-FACE
WITH OPTION TO DIE
MURDER FOR ART'S SAKE
SQUIRE OF DEATH
MURDER CAN'T WAIT
MURDER ROUNDABOUT

Other Books by Richard Lockridge

ONE LADY, TWO CATS
A MATTER OF TASTE
THE EMPTY DAY
ENCOUNTER IN KEY WEST
MR. AND MRS. NORTH

Books by Frances and Richard Lockridge

Cats

CATS AND PEOPLE

Mr. and Mrs. North

MURDER BY THE BOOK
MURDER HAS ITS POINTS
THE JUDGE IS REVERSED
MURDER IS SUGGESTED
THE LONG SKELETON
VOYAGE INTO VIOLENCE
DEATH OF AN ANGEL
A KEY TO DEATH
DEATH HAS A SMALL VOICE
CURTAIN FOR A JESTER
DEAD AS A DINOSAUR
MURDER COMES FIRST
THE DISHONEST MURDERER
MURDER IS SERVED
UNTIDY MURDER
DEATH OF A TALL MAN
MURDER WITHIN MURDER
PAYOFF FOR THE BANKER
KILLING THE GOOSE
DEATH TAKES A BOW
HANGED FOR A SHEEP
DEATH ON THE AISLE
MURDER OUT OF TURN
A PINCH OF POISON
THE NORTHS MEET MURDER
MURDER IN A HURRY

Captain Heimrich

THE DISTANT CLUE
FIRST COME, FIRST KILL
—WITH ONE STONE
SHOW RED FOR DANGER
ACCENT ON MURDER
PRACTISE TO DECEIVE
LET DEAD ENOUGH ALONE
BURNT OFFERING
DEATH AND THE GENTLE BULL
STAND UP AND DIE
DEATH BY ASSOCIATION
A CLIENT IS CANCELED
FOGGY, FOGGY DEATH
SPIN YOUR WEB, LADY!
I WANT TO COME HOME
THINK OF DEATH

Mystery Adventures

THE DEVIOUS ONES
QUEST OF THE BOGEYMAN
NIGHT OF SHADOWS
THE TICKING CLOCK
AND LEFT FOR DEAD
THE DRILL IS DEATH
THE GOLDEN MAN
MURDER AND BLUEBERRY PIE
THE INNOCENT HOUSE
CATCH AS CATCH CAN
THE TANGLED CORD
THE FACELESS ADVERSARY

A PLATE OF RED HERRINGS

BY RICHARD LOCKRIDGE

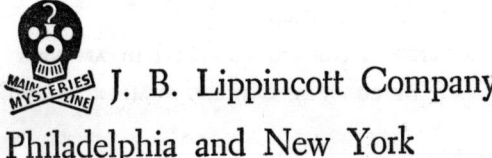 J. B. Lippincott Company

Philadelphia and New York

COPYRIGHT © 1968 BY RICHARD LOCKRIDGE
ALL RIGHTS RESERVED
FIRST EDITION
PRINTED IN THE UNITED STATES OF AMERICA
LIBRARY OF CONGRESS CATALOG NUMBER 68-19830

For Hildy

A PLATE OF RED HERRINGS

I

The party was set for a Friday afternoon in early July. The timing was accepted with a notable lack of enthusiasm by most of those who were expected to attend. Friday afternoons are, almost by definition, short afternoons in summer; it is understood that there will be time in them for a round of golf or a set or two of tennis or for the driving of a power mower over suburban lawns. Those who normally ride out of town on the five-o-eight often make the three-thirty-seven.

Kent Simpson told his wife in New Canaan that God knew when he'd make it and added, "God and UBN," and, being asked, assured her that he sure as hell couldn't give it a miss. Loretta Blaine told her maid that she wouldn't be home for dinner and would grab a bite at the party if she was up to a bite, which she rather doubted. "And," she said, "don't let Tobias con you. Half a jar is quite enough for him, but he'll try to take advantage." Stella said, "Yes'm. I know that cat." Tobias said, "Yowuh." Robert Fremont told the sister with whom he lived on the upper West Side that he did not at all expect to have a good time but that his duty was clear and that, yes, he would drink only sherry, if they had sherry. Being admonished—Ruth Fremont was inclined to admonish her younger brother—Fremont said he was quite aware of his obligation to set a good example. H. R. Stubbs told Mrs. H. R. Stubbs in Plainfield that he had no idea why he was being roped in with the geniuses and would, on the whole, rather not try to guess.

Nora Curran said, "I'll try to be in the apartment by

seven, Bernie. I'm small fry and probably nobody will notice. But it seems to be sort of a command performance."

"Ring out the old, ring in the new," Bernard Simmons said. "And also the one about the king being dead. I'll be sitting on your doorstep at seven."

Martha Scotleigh said, "I know they say he is, dear. But it has to have the wine in it all the same, Mr. Colley or no Mr. Colley. He doesn't have to eat it, except that he probably won't notice if he does. He can eat beef or turkey or whatever. Or the cold salmon, which would be appropriate, wouldn't it? From what we hear."

"I'll make suitable noises, Colley," Jefferson Meade said, in his big corner office on the thirty-sixth floor of the glass shaft on Park Avenue in the Fifties. "As I did to the press when it was announced. As I did in the last installment of 'The Editor's Notebook.' That I look forward with confidence to the future of *The Guardian*. That I am certain it will be revitalized when shaped by younger hands yet will keep unchanged the character which generations of Americans have learned to count on. I'm quoting myself correctly, Colley?"

Bryan Colley sat in a red leather arm chair on the wrong side of Meade's desk. He managed to sit upright in the deep chair, which was something of a trick. He said, "We all felt you expressed it perfectly, Mr. Meade. Particularly the bit a little later on about the continuity being maintained."

"Oh, I'm a pro," Meade said. "An old pro, but a pro. Or—an old swan, Colley?"

Bryan Colley said he didn't get it. He had a quick crisp voice.

"Singing a song," Jefferson Meade said. "Inaudible to the —what is the age range, Colley? Eighteen to thirty? Is that it?"

"Twenty to thirty-five, Mr. Meade," Colley said. "What we plan to shoot at. Young women—men too, of course—on their way up. Starting out in life."

"New and improved," Meade said. "I read the ads, Colley. Even look at the commercials. The other evening I looked at an hour and a half of commercials, interrupted occasionally by snatches from an old movie. The plot seemed to be that cigarettes are getting longer and longer."

Bryan Colley smiled, narrowly.

"The improvement escapes me," Meade said. He took a pack of cigarettes out of his jacket pocket and shook cigarettes loose in it and held the pack across the desk to the erect, younger man. Colley said, "Thanks, no, Mr. Meade. I don't—"

"Forgot," Meade said, and used a desk lighter. "Or drink, I understand?"

"Or drink, Mr. Meade."

"New and improved too," Meade said. "Very commendable. I'll mention how continuity is to be maintained. To the staff, at the party. Have you started to tell them yet, Colley?"

"Not yet."

"Selfishly," Meade said, "I'm glad you're taking it on, Colley. I've known most of them for a good while. Brought some of them here myself. Approved all of them, of course. They'll get a fair shake?"

"A month's pay at the least," Colley said. "More for the ones with seniority, of course. And where retirement is agreed on, UBN is assuming the obligation. The board is being entirely fair. I might even say scrupulously fair."

"Might you, Colley? Yes, I suppose you might. The lawyers haggled long enough. I—"

He stopped speaking. He looked around the big corner office—looked across his heavy desk at thick curtains which dropped from ceiling to floor, at the leather-covered chairs which glowed deeply red, at the leather sofa which matched the chairs. He did not look at Bryan Colley. When he spoke it was more to himself than to Colley.

"Anachronistic," he said. "From another day and another place. From the old building. Out of place here. Sedate here. But the curtains do keep out the sun."

He looked at Colley, then.

"New and improved," he said. "A building three fourths glass. And the heaviest possible curtains to keep the sun out because without them the air conditioning can't make it. On lower Fifth there were thick walls and windows you could open.

Of course, in those days, you could breathe the air. You didn't know the old building, did you, Colley?"

"No, Mr. Meade," Colley said. "Only from outside, that is. A very dignified building."

"Old-fashioned," Meade said. "The elevators took forever. But forty years ago, Colley, I was spry enough to walk upstairs." He looked around the room again. "Some of these things," he said, "were in the founder's office. Liked to be called the founder, Mr. Craigie did."

Bryan Colley did not say anything. He did look at the watch on his wrist.

"Boring you," Meade said. "Boring myself, come to that."

He stood up behind his desk. He was a tall, spare man; he had white hair and a trimmed white mustache and he was tanned from weekends on golf courses and on the Sound. He said, "All right, Colley. It's about time for the wake."

Nora Curran switched the machine on, as the last of the odds and ends she had spent the afternoon clearing up, and spoke into the mouthpiece. She said, "Mr. George Madden and the rest of it. Dear George, Thanks for letting us have a look at Brett Smith's new one and I'm sorry Kent has decided it isn't for us. Personally, I thought it moved right along, but Kent says he wasn't hooked and doesn't think our readers would be either. So, sorry, my dear. One of these days, when things quiet down here, I'd love to take you up on the drink offer. Make that a P.S., Mary. No, skip it. I'll write it in. And make it 'Assistant to the Fiction Editor,' Mary. Mr. Simpson likes it that way. I'll sign it Monday."

She clicked the machine off, having clicked off Mr. Brett Smith, who wouldn't know it until his agent got around to telling him, probably in mid-week. But Smith was used to that sort of thing. If he wasn't, he was in the wrong trade. Hook or get left hanging on a hook. Particularly nowadays. At least one other magazine—*Craddock's*, at a guess; *Craddock's* paid as well as anybody—had had a look at Brett Smith's suspense novel. The carbon manuscript was smudged a little.

She read down the notes she had penciled on her desk pad and checked them off, item by item, during the afternoon. "Biog N.B." Check mark. "Call Dr. Werkes." Check mark. (The check after that was a ragged one, as if the fingers which had made it had trembled.) "See K.S. re A issue." Check mark. (Kent Simpson had said, "I'm damned if I know, Nora. Word hasn't come down.") It was a rather long column of directions to herself. The next to the last notation was, "Party 5." (The last was entirely personal and essentially unnecessary. It was "Bernie 7 if can make.")

It was twenty minutes after five when Nora Curran, assistant fic—no, assistant to the fiction editor—put a cover on her typewriter and wondered, with vague apprehension, if she would ever take it off again. She shook apprehension off—tried to shake it off. She went down the corridor and opened the door with the sign "Powder Room" projecting above it.

Inside, Martha Scotleigh said, "Hi, kid." Nora Curran said, "Hello, Mrs. Scotleigh."

"Goodies," Martha Scotleigh said. "Hot and cold goodies. UBN will be proud of its test kitchen."

"Everybody always has been," Nora said, and sat in front of a mirror to put on a new face.

"We slave over hot stoves," Martha said. "We kitchen test and kitchen test. We tempt eight million palates monthly."

"Last issue, only seven and a half," Nora said, and started to put a new mouth on. "*Craddock's* had eight and a half. And heaven knows how many more color pages."

"The United Broadcasting Network will provide," Martha Scotleigh said. "The United Broadcasting Network is all things to all people."

Mrs. Scotleigh, food editor of *The Guardian*, used that as an exit line.

It wasn't much of one, Nora thought, watching the sturdy departure—and thinking, in parenthesis, that the summer suit skirt she saw receding in the mirror was too smoothly tight on a girdled behind. She returned to her own face; looked hard at the delicately defined bones of cheek and jaw and thought that she was losing weight and that her face, in recent months, had begun to look drawn. From, she thought, not sleeping enough. She ran a comb through shining short brown hair and realized that she was as ready as she'd ever be to join the party which celebrated, if it could be called that, the closing of the final issue of *The Guardian* under the old management. The A issue—at *The Guardian* the immediately impending issue was always the "A issue"—would be published, as before, by The Home Guardian Corporation. But in the statement of ownership, packed tight in four-point type, there would be further identification—"The Home Guardian Corporation, a subsidiary of the United Broadcasting Network."

She stood up and pulled a blue linen dress smooth over hips and buttocks which did not need to be girdled in.

Martha's exit line didn't sparkle, Nora Curran thought. It was merely true. Or, certainly, on the way to becoming true. "Diversifying" was one word for what UBN was about. "Gobbling" was another.

Radio and television stations, owned and affiliated, across the country—that was what UBN basically was about. But UBN now—for some ten years now—had spread far beyond its base. Nora had looked UBN up when rumors first trickled to her small-fry level. A newspaper in California and another in Utah. "Communications," still, in the accepted word. Stretch the word a little and it would cover United Records, Inc., which had been the Eliot Recording Company; stretch it further and it might, she supposed—beginning as she walked along a hallway to hear party babble—wrap partly around Northeast Electric, which did make, among other things, television sets. And it was easy to fit into the word "Communications" Wilson & Blake, Publishers, and Materson & Brothers, who also were publishers and hadn't, for a hundred and fifty years, needed to mention it. And the Zenith Studios, in Hollywood, also fitted in; UBN had discovered that viewers liked old movies and so had now begun to make them, fresh.

Nora turned left into a wider corridor, and as she faced the open doors of the *Guardian* library—usually churning with people from Research—the party sounds stopped. She stopped, too, just outside the doors. Jefferson Meade, erect and spare, white-haired and white-mustached, unwrinkled in a light gray summer suit, was standing at the end of the library, and Bryan Colley was standing beside him. Colley was shorter than Meade. He had black hair. He was almost as tanned of face as the older man, but his tan was somehow less convincing.

"To give you all a chance to meet Mr. Colley," Meade was saying as Nora stopped just outside the library turned party room. "Our new executive editor. I imagine you all know of him—of his outstanding record with what now is—" Meade stopped for a moment, and it seemed to Nora that he swallowed. "Our parent company," Meade went on, after the most momentary of hesitations.

Bryan Colley looked, modestly, over the heads of the forty or so men and women who almost crowded the big reference-book-lined room. He was a trimly muscular man in a very dark gray suit. He has, Nora Curran thought, the sharpest face I've ever seen. She returned to listening.

"—less direct control over the operation," Meade was saying, and Nora assumed he was speaking of his own new role. "And I'm sure you'll all cooperate with Mr. Colley as you have with me. As some of you have for a good many years with me. Mr. Colley tells me that he—the United Broadcasting Network—has certain changes in mind. But that they will be made gradually; that nothing will interrupt the continuity of *The Guardian*—essentially change the place it has made for itself in the American scene."

Rather suddenly it occurred to Nora Curran that Jefferson Meade, for so many years "the chief," was satirizing his own words as he, rather elaborately, chose them. She had only met him once, although often he had gravely and smilingly nodded to her, and had no real idea what his normal idiom was. She doubted that it often included "the American scene." If I were editing, she thought, I'd capitalize the "S" in "scene."

"—confident things will work themselves out," Meade was saying. "And that most of you would rather have a drink than a speech. Would myself. Unless Mr. Colley?"

He let it hang there. Colley looked, Nora thought, slightly surprised. But surprise, if it existed, was momentary.

"Nothing to add, chief," Colley said. "Glad to be here, is all. Have to feel my way along for a while, and I know all of you'll help. Teach me the ropes."

He smiled at them. He had a narrow smile on a sharp face. He had, also, a crisply sharp voice. He did not, to Nora, sound particularly like a man who thought he would need to be taught any ropes.

"Meanwhile," said Bryan Colley, former program coordinator of the United Broadcasting Network, as of this afternoon executive editor of *The Home Guardian*—the word "home" in the title had eroded with the years—"Meanwhile, have fun." It sounded to Nora Curran, as she went on into the library, more like a directive than an invitation.

The small desks for researchers had been herded out of the library. Small tables replaced them. A trestle table stretched along one side wall. It was covered with a white tablecloth which dropped, in front, to the floor; bottles were ranked on it and behind it three men in white jackets waited. A similar table along the opposite wall had three men under chefs' hats behind it and food on it. There was, when Nora Curran joined the party, nobody in front of this table but Martha Scotleigh, who was walking along it, obviously as inspector. She pointed at one platter and the nearest man in a chef's hat turned the platter around.

While Jefferson Meade assured them that the continuity of *The Guardian* would remain uninterrupted, most of the people who crowded the big room had been grouped between the trestle tables, a captive audience. Being directed to have fun, most of them turned to the bar. A few who had been early, and foresighted, carried drinks to tables.

Nora went toward the bar, sorting her way between tables, saying "Hi" and "Good evening" and "Hello, there," as seemed suitable. It was suitable, for example, to say "Good evening" to Robert Fremont, religious editor of *The Guardian*, at present responsible for the "You and Your God" pieces which had appeared monthly for seventy years or so. "Hi" did for Loretta Blaine, although she was art director and hence very senior.

As she worked her way into the party, Nora realized that, while she knew some of the people who made it, she did not know them all; did not know a good many of them even by sight. Most of these, the strangers, were at the end of the bar farthest from the door. They seemed to cluster together, as if they were having a party of their own. As she waited, four layers from the bar, Nora saw that one of this almost withdrawn group was Bryan Colley; it occurred to her that these outsiders, these non-members of the staff, clustered around Colley.

She did not try to push her way toward the bar. Late at the party, she felt herself not yet of it and felt there was no special need to hurry into it. She was content to let it clatter around her. It did clatter. It clattered more like the second hour of a cocktail party than like the first.

Most of them had, Nora thought, taken their Friday afternoons, command party or no command party. They had, almost certainly, taken it at Vittori's, which, that month of that year, was the restaurant at which they lunched—at which, by tradition, they lunched longest when the issue was (finally) put to bed.

It was a shrill party, Nora Curran thought, standing still on the edge of it—standing as one might stand at the edge of a turbulent pool, or a breaking sea, bracing for the first contact. There was animation and a good deal of laughter, and most of the laughter was pitched unnaturally high. For a moment, Nora was tempted to turn away from the party, to walk out on the party. But that wouldn't do. The word had been passed—passed, evidently, to all at *The Guardian* who had appropriate status. Even, she thought, assistant status, as she had. Percy Winnick, who was herdsman for the staff—who was editorial office manager—had passed the word. Mr. Meade would appreciate it if everybody showed up.

Showing and immediately going away wouldn't do. Stay

and have fun and, if Bryan Colley decided to circulate, be cordial to Bryan Colley. So—

She edged into the crowd around the long bar. The trouble was, as the trouble always is, that those who had got their drinks stayed close to the bar to drink them. "Please," Nora said to the left shoulder of Rosalie Shaffner, fashion editor. Rosalie moved the shoulder slightly, creating a gap of some six inches. "Please," Nora said and then, "Oh, Mr. Simpson. Did I bump you?"

Kent Simpson was a substantial man to bump. He was a solidly heavy man. He said, "You're too little, girl. Where's your drink?"

"I'm working toward it," Nora said.

"Too little," Simpson said again. His words slurred somewhat and it was unlike Kent Simpson to slur words. He was precise with words, as authors of fiction frequently discovered. It occurred to Nora that the fiction editor to whom she was assistant had lunched at Vittori's.

"Here," Simpson said, and thrust his highball glass out toward her. It was a full glass. More or less involuntarily, Nora took the glass. She also said, "But—"

"Find us a table, child," Simpson said. "Take my drink to it and I'll get you one. What?"

"A martini, if they run to that," Nora said. "But there's no reason you should—"

"Run to everything," Simpson said. "Courtesy of UBN. Find us a table, child." It sounded rather like "chile" as, Nora thought, in "honey chile." She knew that this substantial boss of hers had come from somewhere in the South—as she knew that he had been a wrestler in college and, for some years, a highly successful writer of highly popular short stories. In almost two years of assisting him she had never before heard the South in his speech.

He went toward the bar, saying "Sorry" at intervals, and advancing, for all his regrets, rather like a bulldozer. Nora carried his drink down the room to a table which would hold two drinks. Nobody was making much use of tables and that, passingly, made her think of Bernie Simmons. "Never stand up when you can sit down" was Bernie's stated and, when possible, adhered-to rule.

Kent Simpson was quick, and he carried a squat glass of pale liquid with a sliver of lemon peel floating on top of it.

"On the rocks," he said, and put the glass on the table. "Up would slosh." He sat down firmly on a small chair. "A brawl," he said. "An ever-loving brawl. Only not so all-fired loving. You scared, lady?"

"Scared?"

"The moving finger, Nora. Represented by a Miss Pickett. Pickett, I give you my word."

Nora repeated a name which meant nothing to her.

"The finger," Simpson said. "As in put the finger on. Goes along with Colley. First assistant sadist."

Nora shook her head and sipped from her glass. The martini was sharp on her tongue. Kent Simpson looked thoughtfully at his glass instead of continuing. He lifted his glass and took a large swallow from it. She said, "I don't know what you mean, Mr. Simpson. Sadist?"

"All right," Simpson said. "Hatchet man, if you'd rather. Colley, that is. Same thing when they took over Materson's. The way Colley likes to do it. What he seems to get a kick out of. The personal touch. Like putting pins through butterflies and watching them wriggle. Sense of power. Instead of putting it in writing."

He's really had a good deal to drink, Nora thought. He is always concise; now he's rambling—now, so far as she could see, he was not making any special sense. She tried to redirect him. She said, "Materson's?"

"And Brothers," Simpson said, speaking more or less into his glass. "Not that there have been any Matersons in the firm for a couple of generations." He looked up from his glass and looked at her rather sharply. "The publishers," he said. "Diversified into UBN couple of months ago."

That, at any rate, was clear. She knew that UBN had absorbed Materson & Brothers. Or, as the announcement said, "bought a controlling interest." She knew and told Kent Simpson she knew.

"Guy I knew there," he said. "Been there for ages. Hell of a good editor. Worked with his writers. If he thought they had something worth digging for. Weren't just the quickie boys and girls."

Again he interrupted himself to drink.

"Had a going-away party there too," he said. "Tribute to old Osgood, who'd carried on the traditions for so many years. Earned his retirement. Gold watch to the departing. All the usual crap." He stopped abruptly. He said, "Sorry. X it out, Miss Curran."

Nora smiled faintly. She was tempted to say she knew all the words and resisted the temptation.

"In the red, of course," Simpson said. "Needed new money, as well as new blood. Materson and Brothers, I mean. Same like *The Guardian*. Osgood had a chance at *The Girl Friends* and turned it down. Said it was lurid trash. And Slade Associates brought it out and made God knows what. Best-seller list for damn near a year. And—"

Again he stopped abruptly, but the interruption this time was not his own.

Two people were standing over them. One was Percy Winnick, who did not stand at all high over them. Winnick was short and slight and had gray hair brushed thinly over a bald head. His expression was harried.

A woman was with him. She was taller and had no lack of hair, hers black. She wore a sleek black dress and very high heeled black shoes. She did not in the least teeter on her spikey heels. She was, Nora decided, in her mid-thirties and polished to stay there.

Winnick had a harried voice, to go with his expression. He said, "Sorry to butt in, Kent. Miss Curran. Want you both to meet Miss Pickett. Mr. Colley's assistant. Kent Simpson, our fiction editor, Miss Pickett. And Miss Curran. Miss—" He hesitated.

Nora gave him the name that went with Curran.

"So glad," Miss Pickett said. There was a minimum of gladness in her voice. "When you're free, Mr. Simpson, Mr. Colley would like a few minutes of your time."

She looked down at Simpson's glass, which was half empty.

"When you finish your drink," Miss Pickett said.

Kent Simpson shrugged heavy shoulders. He finished his drink. He stood up. He said, "I'll go quietly, Miss Pickett," and did go—quietly and with marked steadiness—after the dark-haired woman, who had no difficulty whatever in leading a way through the party. It seemed to part to let her pass.

II

She sat at the small table, her drink half finished, and let the party swirl around her. She watched groups form and break apart; she watched Martha Scotleigh heartily slap Robert Fremont on the back and saw Fremont stagger slightly. But perhaps, she thought, he did not stagger solely because of Martha's heartiness. "We who are about to die," somebody —some man—said loudly from the center of a group. He said the familiar words with a kind of triumph, as if he had just put them together. Rosalie Shaffner, who usually looked every inch a fashion editor, had somewhat lost control of her hair, which usually was so obedient to the whims of her hairdresser. (A different whim each three or four days.) Rosalie was talking, with marked animation, to two of the men who, earlier, had clustered together around Bryan Colley—two of the carefully barbered, tensely pulled-together men of the group she had never seen before.

The bar was not so impossibly surrounded. By ones and twos the staff members, and some of the strangers, had burrowed across the library to the food table and were foraging. Miss Pickett, as remotely graceful as before, came into the room through one of the doors at the far end and went among those still at the bar. She spoke to someone there, but Nora could not tell to whom she spoke. She came out again, and came alone.

Nora sat on the outskirts of the party and looked at it vaguely and could neither join it nor, in any real sense, keep her mind on it. She found she was, dimly, missing somebody who should be at the party and could not decide who was missing, who should be in the center. Then, suddenly, she could. Jefferson Meade was not visible; it appeared that he was playing hooky from his own party. If, of course, it was really his party. And Bryan Colley was missing too. He—of course. He was somewhere having a few words with Kent Simpson. About the A issue, which would be the October issue, appearing in latish September.

"Sitting this one out?" Molly Finch, assistant art director, asked down to her. Molly wore an orange dress which was shaped like an uncontrolled balloon. She held a highball glass, which from its color contained Scotch, and waved it gently in front of Nora. It splashed a little.

"Taking a breather," Nora told Molly Finch, who appeared to regard this as a satisfactorily relevant answer and went away. She did not go far alone. Kenneth Lord (architecture) put an arm around her shoulders in a hug. Ken Lord was the hugging type. He hugged Molly toward the bar, gesturing with his free hand, which held an empty glass. And a square-shouldered man with thick gray hair stopped in front of her and looked at her intently, but seemingly without recognition. Nora did not recognize him, either, but felt vaguely—that day all her feelings and thoughts were dim—that she had seen him before. His identity, or part of it, came to her. She had seen him several times on one of the elevators and he had got out of the car on the floor below, which was shared by the test kitchens and the advertising department. Under the control of Jefferson Meade, business and editorial personnel did not mingle.

H. R. Stubbs, advertising manager, produced a woodenish smile and a stiff nod of the head and went toward the food table.

A waitress in uniform carried a tray of used glasses to Nora's table and stopped and said, "May I, miss?" and, assuming an answer, picked up Kent Simpson's empty glass and put it with the other empty glasses, many of which had lipstick on their rims. A waiter, in a short black uniform jacket, stopped with another tray. The glasses on it were filled. He held it toward Nora and Nora said, "Thank you, no," and he bowed slightly and carried the drinks into the swirl of the party.

And a man swirled out of it and, without saying anything at all, pulled out the chair which had been Kent Simpson's and sat on it and put an old-fashioned glass down on the table with a clunk. Then he began, slowly, to shake his head.

His head was too large for the rest of him. He had a very high forehead which rose straight up from his eyebrows for an unexpected number of inches and then went almost straight back. He had a fringe of red hair which went around his head like a hedge and he had a red mustache.

"Seen you around here," he said, very suddenly just as Nora had decided he did not see her at all. "You the one who swiped my office?"

She looked at him, knowing she looked blankly. She shook her head and had a feeling that, in some hypnosis, she was moving her head in time with his.

"Armstrong," the man said. He had a heavy voice—a voice more suitable to his massive head than to the rest of him, which was scant. "Clifford Armstrong." When he gave his name he gave it curtly, as if it should not have been necessary to give it at all.

So this is Clifford Armstrong, she thought. Dr. Clifford Armstrong. And somebody had swiped his office. "Not I," Nora said. "Swiped?"

"Books," Armstrong said. "Notes. Everything. Except the manuscript itself. Had the sense to take that home with me. Where's Meade?"

"Mr. Meade was here," Nora said. "I haven't seen him for—oh, half an hour or so."

Armstrong kept on shaking his heavy head. The movement reminded her of something and she tried to think what it was and it came to her. He moved his head, and his shoulders with it, like a bull preparing to charge a matador. She had seen motion pictures of angry, uncertain bulls. She had been sorry for the bulls. But Clifford Armstrong, sitting across from her, did not look like a man to be sorry for.

She knew about him. All the staff knew about him, although he was not a member of the staff—not properly a member. He had an office on the editorial floor. Or, as it now appeared, had had.

He had been in and out, apparently usually at night, for several years. He was what Kent Simpson had once called "our historian in residence." He was an historian of considerable, perhaps of great, reputation. He was working, on assignment, with annual advances—the amounts of which members of the staff had frequently guessed at aimlessly—on a book which Jefferson Meade had commissioned and which *The Guardian* was to print. (Some said in its entirety.)

"A pet project of the chief's," Simpson had told her. "Part of the continuity he's always talking about. 'We, the Inheritors.' That's what it's going to be called. If Armstrong ever finishes it. Apparently, what this generation owes to this country's past. With suitable illustrations thereof. How the past has shaped the present, whether the present appreciates it or not. Something the chief is hipped on."

Nora had said it sounded a bit heavy for the present-day *Guardian*, which for some years now had tried, a little anxiously, not to be heavy.

"Armstrong is supposed to be witty, as historians go," Simpson had told her. "Anyway, the chief thinks so, and he's read a couple of Armstrong's books and I haven't. Anyway, *The Guardian*'s put a good deal into advances and given the old boy all the time he needs to come through. Given him the use of an office. So that, when his kids drive him nuts, he can work here instead of at home. About this story of Norton's, I'm afraid it's no. See why you liked it, but—"

As he sat across from her and moved his doleful—or threatening—head, Clifford Armstrong did not look like a man who would have children young enough to drive him nuts. Perhaps Simpson had meant grandchildren.

Armstrong stopped moving his head from side to side. He leaned forward and put his elbows on the little table, which tilted momentarily. He put his hands up to his big head, as if to support its weight or quiet its movement. He looked intently at Nora Curran.

"By the way," he said, "who are you?"

She told him who she was and what she was on *The Guardian*.

"Don't look it," Armstrong said.

That had been said to Nora before, under gayer circumstances. It hadn't made any particular sense then, either. Now she said, "Is an associate editor supposed to look a special way, Dr. Armstrong?"

"Harried," he said. "And you sit here moping. What's this damn brawl all about? I come down here to work and find a brawl."

"A tribute to Mr. Meade," Nora said. "At least, I guess that's it. Or a welcome to the United Broadcasting Network."

He drank from his glass and took his elbows off the table and began to shake his head again.

"Come down here to work," Armstrong said. "Find my office cleaned out. Go to Meade's office to find out what the hell and the door's locked. Go next door to Barclay's office and the door opens all right and there's a man inside talking on the telephone but it isn't Barclay. And then I hear yelling out here."

"Mr. Barclay isn't here any more," Nora said. "He left two weeks ago." She thought for a moment. "About the time the new ownership was announced. They say he's going over to *Craddock's*."

"Never see it," Armstrong said. "Never saw *The Guardian* either, until Meade got in touch with me."

He leaned forward again.

"And," he said, "persuaded me to leave the faculty, *and* tenure, and take on this project of his. Know about that?"

"A little," Nora said. "It's—word of it's trickled down, Dr. Armstrong. It sounds very interesting. The present's unrecognized debt to the past."

"Way of putting it," Armstrong said. "One way of putting it. Give the twerps an inkling. Not the way Meade put it, but what he meant. Continuity, he called it. Talked a lot about continuity. Only, where's mine?"

"Probably," Nora said, "they're just moving people

around. Into new offices, I mean. Probably that's all it is, Dr. Armstrong."

"Enough to live on," Armstrong said. "The way an educator learns to live. But drops in the bucket. For a man like me a sizable bucket, the way Meade promised. And so now this broadcasting outfit takes over and what about Meade? Eased out, Miss Curran?"

"The way it seems to be," she said, "Mr. Meade stays on as editor. A Mr. Colley takes over as executive editor. It was probably Mr. Colley you saw in the office next to Mr. Meade's when you were looking—"

He interrupted.

"You said Colley?" he said. "You mean Bryan Colley?"

"Yes."

"That son of a bitch," Dr. Clifford Armstrong, former professor of history at a small, but highly regarded, Western college, said to Nora Curran. Then he got up and went away, carrying his drink.

It was not, Nora thought, a day when anything, or anybody, made particular sense. Nor, she thought, looking at her watch and seeing it was a quarter after six, does my being here. If I leave now—

She stood up. Standing, she had a better view of the party, which now seemed to be dwindling. She had, also, a view of Kent Simpson as he came in through one of the doors at the end of the room.

He came heavily, and Nora thought that the heaviness was more than physical. For so big a man, Kent Simpson had always seemed to her to move almost lightly. Now he did not. He passed Rosalie Shaffner and Nora thought that the fashion editor—whose hair still was more or less going its own way—said something to him, and smiled at him. But Simpson did not seem to hear her if she spoke, or to see her. He plodded on toward Nora Curran at the table they had shared.

There was, of course, no real reason he should. Certainly there was no reason for him to come back and join her. Of course, if Colley had wanted to see him about fiction for the A issue, or for subsequent issues, it would have been natural for Simpson to pass the word on to her. If there was a word to be passed it was, evidently, going to wait until Monday. So there was no reason she shouldn't slip out of a party she had never really joined. Leaving now, and having any luck with a taxi—which was as unlikely as anything she could think of— she could get to her apartment and change and freshen and be ready when the doorbell rang.

She walked toward the main door, with a smile ready for any who smiled at her. Her progress was slow; a good many smiled at her and spoke to her and she gave them smile for smile and words for inconsequential words. Finally she reached the door and Miss Pickett, as darkly groomed as ever (nothing had happened to her hair), was standing near it. Miss Pickett smiled, sharply.

"Not leaving already, Miss Curran?" Miss Pickett said and her voice, like her smile, was sharp. "So soon?"

"I have a slight head—" Nora said and Miss Pickett, not waiting for the obvious, said she was so sorry but that she did hope Miss Curran would stay a little longer.

"Because," Miss Pickett said, "Mr. Colley would like to see you for a few minutes before you go and he's not free at the moment. So if you could?"

There was only one thing to say. "Of course," Nora Curran said, and went back into the party.

This time she went to the bar. Kent Simpson did not appear to be at it. She looked across the room toward the buffet table. Kent Simpson did not appear to be there, either. She said, "Could I have a martini, please?" to the bar man. She got a martini and moved away from the bar and Kenneth Lord said, "Over here, honey," and she went over there, one place being as good as another, and sat with Kenneth Lord and Molly Finch and sipped a drink she did not want, and heard and said words she did not listen to.

It was almost seven when Miss Pickett came up to them —glided up to them, Nora thought.

"I'm so sorry you've had to wait, Miss Curran," Miss Pickett said. "Mr. Colley is free now."

Nora followed Miss Pickett, who had no trouble gliding

through the thinned-out party. Smiles and inconsequential words did not impede Miss Pickett's progress. There were none.

Miss Pickett opened the door of the office, which had been Nelson Barclay's. She said, "Miss Nora Curran, Mr. Colley," and Nora went into the office. Miss Pickett closed the door after her from the outside.

She let herself out the "back door" and walked the corridor, her heels clicking on the polished tile floor. She turned the familiar corridor and stood, alone, in the space between the two banks of elevators, six on either side. All the elevators seemed, from their signals, to be going up. She pressed a "down" button and waited, still alone in a space which, a couple of hours ago, must have been crowded.

An elevator showed its red "down" signal and she moved to it and waited. And then, hurrying, a slight man with thinning blond hair came into the elevator corridor and joined her to wait for the elevator. She said, "Good evening, Mr. Fremont," to Robert Fremont, sometimes referred to—behind his back—as "Rev-Rob."

The elevator stopped and she went into it and pressed the button numbered "1," which lighted up. Fremont came in behind her and looked at her, she thought dazedly. Then he said, "Oh, good evening, Miss Curran." He had a light, uncertain voice.

The elevator door closed and the car began to plunge down.

"It was quite a party, wasn't it?" Fremont said, in the tone of someone who feels that something ought to be said. She agreed, in much the same tone, that it had been quite a party. The indicator lighted from floor to floor as each floor was passed. The car stopped at the twenty-third, and three men got in and stood between Nora and Robert Fremont. Fremont, who had said all he apparently felt ought to be said, looked at the back of the nearest man. He looked, Nora thought, as if he did not see the back of the man.

From the seventeenth floor the car plunged down to the lobby floor and stopped and the door opened. The four men moved back and Nora went out into the air-conditioned lobby. Fremont followed her and then the others. As she walked toward the exit doors, Fremont walked a few paces behind her, not trying to catch up with her. Then, at the cigar stand, he turned aside and she heard his light voice, which had, for all its lightness, a carrying quality. What she heard was, "Chesterfields, please."

She went on and out of the cool lobby into the city's heat. She had forgotten how hot a day it was—still was, at after seven in the evening. The damp heat pressed down on her. She looked down Park Avenue for a cab with its roof light on. There was only one in sight, but its light spelled "Off Duty."

She was six blocks from home—three shorter blocks south of it and three longer blocks west. She began to walk. Until she reached the first intersecting street, she kept looking back down Park for a cab. As she crossed the street, which was westbound, she looked through it. There was no vacant cab in sight.

She walked on up the avenue. As she walked, she felt she was walking as heavily as Kent Simpson had when he went through the party toward the bar. But I don't weigh half as much as he does, she thought, and the words "half as much, half as much, half as much" beat in her mind, as if a metronome timed them.

She did not walk rapidly; the same metronome seemed to time her steps. It was long after seven. He had said he would be waiting on the doorstep. "Sitting on the doorstep." But there wasn't any doorstep. He knew there wasn't any doorstep. He would have given her up half an hour ago. Or he would have gone somewhere to a telephone and tried to reach her at the office and in her own cubicle the telephone might have rung and rung unanswered. Because she was at the party; having fun at the party.

When she reached her cross-town street she turned right, without actually knowing she turned right. She grazed against a woman and said, "Sorry. My fault. Sorry," without knowing she said the words. At Lexington she stopped and waited for the light to change and at Second she stopped again and waited again. Then she went on, heavily and the meaningless words "half as much, half as much" began again to beat dully in her mind. She turned, finally, into the doorway of the apartment house she lived in.

Fred had his uniform jacket off and was sitting on a straight chair near the door. He had his shirt collar open. He said, "It's sure a hot one, ain't it? Man's been looking for you. Man with red hair. I said I didn't think so but he could go up and try."

It was a day of ellipses. It seemed to her as she walked the dimmer, but not essentially cooler, lobby toward the elevator that all day nobody had ever spelled out a thought, used the words which would complete a thought. (Except Dr. Werkes, she remembered. He had been direct enough; he had spelled things out.) She pressed the button marked "5" and the elevator door closed and the elevator car went up and stopped and opened its door again. She walked down the corridor toward 5J.

A tall thin man with very red hair was leaning against the wall beside the door numbered "5J."

Nora Curran said, "I'm sorry, Bernie. I thought you would have got tired of waiting." She fished in her handbag for her key, and when she got the key out he took it from her and opened the door. "You shouldn't have waited," she said, as she went into the apartment, and was conscious of the dullness in her voice.

It was hot in the apartment. She had turned the room air conditioner off when she left in the morning. She walked across the square living room to the window and turned the air conditioner on. It rattled at first. It always rattled at first, apparently in resentment. Then it began to hum.

Bernard Simmons, assistant district attorney, County of New York, assigned to the Homicide Bureau, went into the room and closed the door after him. He crossed the square living room and looked down at Nora. He looked down from six feet two to five feet four.

"To be honest about it," Bernie Simmons said, "you look beat, darling. It must have been quite a party."

She looked up at him and tried, without much success, to form a smile.

"Yes," she said, "it was quite a party. We stood in line to get fired. He fired the big ones first. What was that Navy saying you used to tell me about, Bernie?"

"Rank hath its privileges," Bernie said. "Sit down before you fall down, Nora. What have you been drinking, darling?"

Nora sat down. She said, "I'm not sure I rem—oh, yes, martinis. What did they do with the aristocrats in the French Revolution? Cooped them up somewhere, all together, and every morning—every some time—a jailer came in with a list. Was that it?"

"Something like that," Bernie said. "And read the names on the list. Yes, something like that. And they all bowed—those on the list, I mean—and were improbably courtly. Depends on who wrote the history, I suppose. Sit still. I know where things are."

He went out of the room to the place where things were. After a time he came back with a pitcher of ice on a tray and a bottle of gin and another of vermouth. He said, "I can't find any lemons, girl. Next time I'll bring them with me." He fished ice from the pitcher and said, as much to himself as to her, "Ought to be kept in the freezing compartment," and poured martinis into the glasses and carried them up the room and put one down on a table beside her chair. Still holding his own full glass, and not spilling anything, he turned a chair so it faced hers and used a foot to move a small table near it. He put his glass on the table and sat in the chair.

"So," he said, "you're not an assistant fiction editor any more."

"Not much of anything at the moment," Nora said.

"Oh, yes," Simmons said. "A most attractive young woman with a future ahead of her. In one form or another, of course. Drink your drink, Nora. And tell your bartender what happened. This man Colley, I suppose?"

She sipped from her glass. It was a better martini than

UBN had provided. Behind her, cooler air began to seep from the conditioner.

"Told to have fun," she said. "Only nobody—almost nobody—seemed to be having it. Called in one by one by a woman in black, so chic it set your teeth on edge, and fired in sequence. I don't know who all. My immediate boss, I'm pretty certain. Poor Mr. Fremont, probably. I don't think the new management is going to go in very heavily for God. And Rosalie Shaffner let her hair fall down, so perhaps—I don't really know, Bernie. Only, I'm out on my ear."

"Odd way to go about it," Simmons said. "Simpler ways. Like slips attached to pay checks."

"Apparently," Nora said, "they've done it this way before. When they took over Materson's. The publishers, you know. It was Bryan Colley then, too. Anyway, Mr. Simpson says it was. And that Colley seems to get a kick out of doing it this way."

"Are people like that," Simmons said. "Not pleasant people, but they're around. We run into them from time to time. What did he say, Nora?"

"That they weren't going to use fiction much any more. That fiction, in magazines, is going out. It is, too. Not all the way out. But *The Guardian*'s always used a good many stories. Not as many serials as in the old days. When I was a girl there was a tree in the back yard—a nice easy tree—and I used to climb up in it and read serials in *The Guardian*. And eat apples."

"And," Bernie Simmons said, "series of short stories. I remember. And articles about which side forks went on and whether it was all right to use place mats or it had to be tablecloths. And whether a nice girl ever let a nice boy kiss her. Before they were nicely married. Drink your drink, nice girl."

But he put his own drink down on the table and got up from his chair and went across to her and leaned down and kissed her. At first her lips did not respond to his. Then, tentatively, they did respond.

They had known each other for some two years—had had dinners together, gone together to the theater and to movies; now and then to cocktail parties like the one at which they had first met. It had been, always, light and casual, with no commitment of any kind. In the past six months or so they had, and it had seemed by chance, been together more frequently. Friends they had in common began to invite them together to parties. "The Binghams," she would say on the telephone, "want me to bring an extra man. Do you happen—?" But they were not, Bernie Simmons was almost sure they were not, drifting toward anything. She was gay and pretty and quick, and seemed to enjoy being with him. Once a week, for the past six months or so. Now and then twice a week. But without commitment. When they kissed, when now and then he put a long arm around her and momentarily held her against him, the contacts were enjoyable but not especially compelling. For Bernie Simmons there had been other girls and, he assumed without asking, for her there had been other men.

But now, as he went back to his chair and picked up his glass, Bernie, to his entire surprise, was conscious of a different feeling toward the girl across from him, sunk in a deep chair and now with her eyes closed. Tenderness. That of course was what he felt. It seemed an active feeling for so normally passive an emotion. But that was what it was. He wanted to go back and kiss her again; vaguely, he thought of times he might have kissed her and had not because kissing her had not seemed especially important. Odd thing to happen out of what he had, without putting such words to it, assumed to be a clear sky. Not, of course, that she hadn't all along been damned attractive.

She opened dark brown eyes. He had not, he realized, particularly noticed her eyes before. Apart from her general attractiveness.

"I'm sorry, Bernie," Nora Curran said. "I'm bushed. Maybe you ought to find yourself brighter company."

That was, obviously, not worth answering.

"You'll get another job," he said. "You've told me yourself it's a game of musical chairs. The music's still playing, lady."

"I don't hear it," Nora said. "I don't hear it at all. Oh, I'll get another job. Eventually. There aren't so many of them around any more. They've taken away a good many of the chairs, you know. Oh, I'll find something. Only, probably at about half as much as they paid me at *The Guardian*."

(That was what the dogged repetition had been about. "Half as much, half as much." Not really about my weight as compared to Kent Simpson's weight. About—)

For a moment, Bernie Simmons was a little puzzled and even a little disappointed. Money was damned important. It was important to everybody. Once or twice he had himself been tempted to get out of what politicians called "public service" and into a niche which paid better. Like, for example, criminal practice with somebody like Abe Levinsky. But it had not occurred to him that money was as important to Nora Curran as, somehow, she now made it appear to be. Not that it isn't important to everybody, he told himself again, and felt he was insisting on the obvious.

"Which," Nora said, "happens to be very important to me at the moment, Bernie."

I didn't say anything, Bernard Simmons thought. I'd better wrap insulation around my mind.

"I told you about Dorothy," she said. "When it—when it first happened. It—" She stopped and picked up her glass and, rather abruptly, drank what was in it.

"It hasn't been anything I wanted to talk about," she said, not looking at the red-haired man with the oddly reddish brown eyes. "Not to anybody. Not even to you."

The qualification surprised Bernie Simmons. Of course, she probably hadn't meant anything by it. Still—

"Yes," he said. "You told me about your sister. And I'm damned sorry about it."

"I saw Dr. Werkes last night," Nora said. "And called him up today. Even he doesn't know how long it will be. Or even—he's honest about it—that she'll ever be all right. Only that there's a better chance—probably a better chance, he's an extremely honest doctor—if she's given very special care. And that her being so young makes the chances better."

"How old is Dorothy?"

"Six years younger than I am. That is—she's twenty. Will be next month. Why do things like that happen to people?"

He didn't know. He said that, come down to it, nobody knew. "We're still guessing about the mind," he said. "The best men in the world are still guessing."

He didn't know what had happened to the mind of Dorothy Curran, Nora's young sister, and Nora's only living kin. He knew what a pretty girl, blonde as her sister was brown-eyed and brown-haired, had tried to do. She had tried to kill herself by jumping out of a fifth floor window in her college dormitory. Her roommate had kept her from jumping. Barely kept her from jumping.

There was no way of explaining what had happened to Dorothy Curran's mind. If Isadore Werkes couldn't explain it, there wasn't much likelihood anybody could. He knew Werkes slightly; he knew a good deal about Isadore Werkes, M.D., psychiatrist, and sometimes consultant to the offices of the District Attorney, County of New York.

"Sometimes," Nora said, "they come out of it, Dr. Werkes says. Perhaps, he says, treatment helps. Nobody, he says, really knows. He says there's a little of the manic depressive in almost everybody, that everybody goes down and up and down and up. Sometimes, in some people, there isn't the control most of us have, and sometimes a psychiatrist can find out why and do something about it. Find out where the block is."

"I know," Simmons said.

"Sometimes," Nora said, "she just sits and stares at nothing. Sometimes she dances when there isn't any music. And sometimes, Bernie, she tries to kill herself."

Nora Curran turned in her chair and put her arms along the back of the chair and her head down in her arms. Her shoulders began to shake and Bernie went to kneel beside the chair and put an arm around the shaking shoulders. He didn't say anything because he couldn't think of anything to say.

After some minutes she said, "I'll be all right, Bernie. I'm sorry to put you through this."

There was something to say to that. "For Christ's sake," Bernie Simmons said.

III

He had had trouble in persuading her to change and come out to dinner. She had said nonsensical things—had said that he should go and she'd open a can of something; had said that she couldn't face anybody at the moment; had said that she was a drip and that nobody wanted to take a drip to dinner. And she had been told, several times over, to come off it. She had even been held and shaken gently. She had also been told that drips were his favorite people. Finally she had said, "Oh, all right. I'll only be a minute." She had been not much over twenty; it was still only a little after eight when they got into a cab. Bernie Simmons had a way of finding taxicabs when there obviously weren't any.

The restaurant he took them to was in the East Fifties. It was small, and there were not many people in it. It was cool and softly lighted and quiet. "Busy most nights," Bernie said. "Not Fridays. Not in the summer." To the waiter he said, "Two martinis. Dry. Up. And very, very cold."

"I don't know whether—" Nora said and shrugged her shoulders under a white, sleeveless dress. "Only I don't seem to feel them. The ones at the party. The one you made at the apartment. I—I just feel numb, Bernie. As if I'd been hit with a mallet. But that's not the martinis, is it?"

"No. Of course not," Bernard Simmons said, with rather more assurance in his voice than in his mind. "You've had a jolt. At a very bad time."

Their drinks came.

"I don't want to load it on you," she said. "I hate to load things on people. It's a drippy thing to do."

"Also," he said, "it sometimes helps. Talking about things sometimes helps. About Dorothy?"

She shook her head, at first. She tasted her drink and said it was a good drink. She felt in her handbag and said, "I left my cigarettes at home," and he gave her a cigarette and lighted it. (She kept her head up when he lighted her cigarette. She didn't lean down, risking hair, as so many women did. He'd noticed that for a long time. Only now did he realize he had noticed it.) He waited, his fingers on the stem of his own glass. The stem was cold.

"Dr. Werkes," she said, "says that some of the state institutions are all right. That there are good people working in them. Only not enough of them. Is that true, Bernie?"

"Yes. True enough."

"But that the best private places are better. Give people a better chance. There's one he knows of he thinks is very good. Only it's expensive. Last night, when I told him to go ahead and get her in, I thought I could swing it. Just swing it. Even this afternoon—I called him this afternoon and he said he'd made the arrangements. Even this afternoon, I thought I could swing it." She ground out her cigarette. The movement was abrupt, almost violent. "Damn this man Colley," she said.

"He's only part of it," Simmons said. "The front of it, in this case. An unpleasant man, obviously. But UBN is most of it, Nora."

She supposed so; supposed that Bryan Colley was merely doing what he was told to do. She said that, anyway, it didn't really matter.

"I'm out on my ear," she said. "That's what matters, isn't it? And I've got a kid sister to take care of and we used up most of the money Dad left getting her through college—part way through college. And—"

She stopped and drank from her glass.

"I hate people who blurt," she said. "Women who cry on shoulders and pity themselves. I hate me, Bernie."

"I don't," Simmons said. "On the contrary. How did this man Colley go about it?"

"Said, 'Sit down, Miss—' and he had to look at a list on the desk to find out what my name was. He found it and said, 'May as well sit down.' I sat down. Then he opened a drawer of the desk and got a check out. He pushed it across the desk to me. It was for what I made in a month. Then he said, 'You get the point, Miss—' and had to wait until he remembered what my name was. Only, I don't think he really did. I think he just wanted me to know how unimportant I was. I started to get up and he said, 'Just a minute, Miss Curran.' He remembered my name that time."

She reached out fingers and Simmons put a cigarette between them. He leaned across the table and lighted it for her. She still didn't dip her head toward the flame. She drew on the cigarette.

"He said, 'Matter of policy, Miss Curran. They tell me your work here has been quite satisfactory. The point is, we're going to cut down on fiction. Way down. Personalities. Issues. Real things. Not make-believe things. Changes in sexual mores. That sort of thing. See what I mean?'

"I said, 'Yes, Mr. Colley. More like *Craddock's*.' That's the magazine that stepped on *The Guardian*'s face, Bernie."

"At the cost," Bernie said, "of a few million dollars. That's the story going around. Why, do you suppose? People cut throats for money. Not the other way around."

"I don't know. Only, advertisers go where it glitters most. Probably the Craddock Corporation expects to get its millions back. Anyway, when I mentioned *Craddock's*, Colley said, 'They're doing all right, Miss Curran,' and then, 'That's all, Miss Curran,' and I didn't say anything. Just got up and got out. There was almost nobody left at the party, then. They were clearing the tables. I thought, He's finished with his list. I was at the bottom of it."

Simmons beckoned a waiter, who came with menus. She looked at hers as if she did not see it. He said, "Did you eat at this party?" and she shook her head. "Then now," he said.

She said, "It all sort of blurs, Bernie. It doesn't matter." In the end he ordered for them both.

"We've talked enough about me," Nora said when the

waiter had thanked them and gone away. "What kind of a day did you have?"

"Took witnesses before a grand jury," he said. "*In re* a kid who killed another kid about a girl. A girl who, at a guess, didn't give a damn about either of them. They'll indict on murder one, probably. The foreman, who likes to take over, sounded like it. And we'll take a plea of second degree, probably. Which, I suspect, is all we'd get in the end. We—"

The head waiter came to their table and said, "Mr. Simmons?" and, when that was agreed to, said that there was a telephone call for Mr. Simmons. To which Mr. Simmons said, "Damn." He pushed the table back.

"A few of us alternate as stand-bys," he said. "Keep ourselves available over weekends. I'll try to cut it short, whatever it is."

He followed the head waiter and they went out of sight. She sat and smoked and wondered at which of the dwindling number of magazines she should start looking. Not *Craddock's*, she thought. Although there had been talk of a shakeup there. There was always talk of shakeups and usually it was informed. And if Nelson Barclay was really going there it might make a difference. One way or the other. It was hard to guess.

Bernard Simmons came back and his red hair was bright even in the dim light. While he was still across the room she noticed his reddish brown eyes were narrowed and that there were vertical lines between his eyebrows, which were as red as his hair. But then he smiled across the room at her and briefly spread his hands in a gesture of dismissal. He sat down and said, "Routine," and "Should we have another?" She said, "Not for me, Bernie," and the waiter wheeled a cart to their table and lighted a fire under a metal tray, and poured into it from bottles. Then he carved a duck, quickly and with assurance, and put pieces of duck into the bubbling liquid in the tray and squeezed oranges over them.

He ate and watched her while she ate and felt again the not passive tenderness he had felt before. She ate most of the duck on her plate, which was a good thing. She ate some of her salad. She was, he hoped, coming out of it a little, and thought that she would need to.

They were on coffee and cigarettes when he decided to get on with it.

"The phone call wasn't really routine, Nora," he said. "Didn't want to jolt you until you'd got some food into you. The man who called was a police lieutenant—a man named Stein. Bryan Colley's been killed, Nora. Cleaning woman found his body about an hour ago. Lying across his desk."

He watched her eyes widen and saw the coffee cup she had just lifted shake in her hand. She put it down in the saucer and for an instant it rattled in the saucer. Then, a little vaguely and in a voice he could just hear across the table, she said, "It wasn't anything to kill him for."

He waited a moment, but she did not go on.

"Somebody thought something was," he said. "Remember anything on his desk, Nora? Any—oh, special sort of thing?"

She shook her head.

"Probably was there," he said. "A fishing trophy. A bronze statue of a fisherman, holding a rod out in front of him. 'Bryan Colley, Master Angler' engraved on the base. You don't remember it?"

Again she shook her head.

"What was used," Simmons told her. "Turned out the fishing rod the fisherman was holding was made of steel. It went into his brain, the M.E. says."

He watched color fade from her face, and saw her hands tighten on the edge of the table. But when he started to reach across the table toward her she shook her head and said, "I'm all right, Bernie." She paused a moment and then said, "Really all right. Only, when I saw him this evening, he looked so—so like a man who expected to live forever."

Whatever he had expected, Bryan Colley had lived less than an hour after Nora had left his office. Supposing she had left it a little after seven? "Yes, about then." His body had been found around eight by the cleaning woman.

"Stein and the rest of them are at the *Guardian* offices," Bernie Simmons said. "Trying to get hold, as a starter, of people who were at the party and might have seen something. Barmen, waiters, and waitresses. Everybody they can lay hands on. And—members of the staff who were there, Nora." He paused and drained his coffee cup.

"I didn't," he said, "tell Johnny Stein that I was having dinner with one of the staff members."

"I went into his office," Nora said. "I got fired and got out. He was all right when I left."

"Of course," Simmons said. "Don't bristle, darling."

She said she wasn't bristling. She said, "But, apparently, I was one of the last people to see him alive."

Simmons admitted that there was that. He said, "Thing is, Johnny would like it if I'd come down and sit in. Sometimes we do that and sometimes we don't. Theory is, the police get what evidence they can. D.A.'s office evaluates it. Decides whether there's enough to charge on. Only sometimes one of us sits in from the start. Helps sometimes."

"You're going to on this?"

"Yes, Nora. Take you home and make you promise to take a sleeping pill and—"

"No," she said. "Some time or other they're going to want to talk to me, aren't they? Question me. There won't be anything I can tell them. Except that the party was a firing party. That I was one of those fired. And that being fired couldn't have come at a worse time. They are going to want to question me?"

"Everybody," Simmons said. "Yes, dear, you."

"And you're going there now? And they're trying to get in touch with staff members?"

"Yes to both."

"Most of the people on the staff—the senior people, not us small fry—live out of the city. It will take time to get in touch with them."

"Probably."

"Then," Nora Curran said, "I may as well get it over,

Bernie. And you—you can say a good word for me, if you want to."

"Many," Bernie Simmons said. "Good words I've just thought of, my dear. So, we may as well go."

They paid and went. Again Bernie Simmons got a cab he waved at. Its roof sign had said "Off Duty." But it swerved in toward the curb and the roof sign changed to "Taxi." It was only a few blocks to the unrelenting tower of glass which housed *The Guardian*. It was thirty-seven floors up in a fast elevator. Heavy double glass doors were lettered: "The Home Guardian. Editorial." A uniformed patrolman stood outside the doors. Another uniformed patrolman stood inside them.

There was a central office with some fifty desks, ordered in columns, in it. "For the smallest of small fry," Nora told Bernie Simmons as they walked through it. "And stenographers, of course."

There was no one in the big open room. At the far end of it double doors stood open, and beyond them there was the sound of movement and of voices. As they walked toward the opening, flash bulbs stabbed beyond it. There was another uniformed man there and, again, Simmons told a uniform who he was. They went out of the open room.

There was a wide corridor out of which offices opened. The corridor was brightly lighted and there were a good many men in it. The photographer was working in the office which had been Nelson Barclay's before it was, rather briefly, the office of Bryan Colley. The door to that office was open and a man in civilian clothes was standing in the doorway, looking in. He turned and looked at them. He was a man with noticeably square shoulders. He had a square face. He said, "Evening, Counselor." He looked at Nora Curran. He said, "Lady with you?"

"Lady's with me, Paul," Simmons said to Detective (1st gr.) Paul Lane. "Didn't know this was your precinct."

"Transferred," Lane said. "The lieutenant got shifted to Homicide North and more or less took me along. He's in what's apparently the big shot's office. Getting background from the big shot. And he'd appreciate it if you sat in, Counselor. About the lady—" He paused. "Don't know about the lady," Lane said.

"The lady," Simmons said, "is—was—a member of the staff. She was at this party they had. We both thought the lieutenant would want to talk to her."

"I'd think so," Lane said. "I'd certainly think so, Counselor."

"Then—" Simmons began, and sounds stopped him. At one end of the long, wide corridor a door opened and Jefferson Meade came out—came, Nora knew, out of his own corner office. Behind him a tall, dark man in a gray suit said, "Appreciate your help, Mr. Meade. Sorry to have had to break in on your dinner." Meade said, "Not important. Compared to this not in the least important. And—"

He stopped as Simmons had stopped, and looked down the corridor. Lieutenant John Stein came out behind Meade and looked down the corridor and Nora and Bernie Simmons turned too and looked toward the man who was shouting. He was shouting, "Take your hands off me! I said, *take your hands off me!*"

The man who wanted hands taken off was slight, almost spindly. He had a very large head and a red mustache. The hands belonged to a uniformed patrolman and one of them was on each shoulder of Dr. Clifford Armstrong, who was being propelled, decisively but without violence, up the corridor. He seemed to be squirming under the compelling hands.

"All right, O'Brien," Detective Lane said, raising his voice slightly.

"Snooping in the offices," Patrolman O'Brien said. "Says it's no business of mine what he's looking for. Tried to run and I thought I'd better stop him. He—"

"It's all right, officer," Meade said, his voice also raised. "You can let go of him. He's—probably he was looking for some papers that belong to him. Was that it, Cliff?"

"You're damn right I was," Armstrong said. His heavy voice resounded from tiled floor and plaster walls. "And what the hell goes on here?"

"What has gone on here is murder," John Stein said.

His voice was not raised at all. "Cliff what, Mr. Meade? Oh—Clifford Armstrong? Let him go, O'Brien."

Patrolman O'Brien let him go. O'Brien stopped but Armstrong came on, toward what had become a group near the open door of the office a man had died in. He came at what was almost a trot. Abruptly, when he was quite close, he stopped and looked at all of them. Except for Nora Curran, he had to look up at them, his disproportionately large head tilted back precariously.

"And who," Clifford Armstrong said, "are all of you? What are they doing here, Meade? I get thrown out of my office and now—" He stopped. Then he said, "Murder? What do you mean, murder?"

"I'm a police officer," Stein said. "Mr. Colley was killed tonight, Professor. At his desk. In there."

Stein gestured toward the office Colley had been killed in.

"For my money," Armstrong said, "he had it coming. He was a son of a bitch of the first water." He paused and nodded his big head. "Dead *or* alive," he said, confirming himself.

"Nobody has it coming," Stein told him and then said, "Hate to break in on your evening, Counselor."

"What my evenings are for, Johnny," Simmons said. "This is Miss Curran, Johnny. She was here earlier and—"

"Good evening, Miss Curran," Stein said. "We tried to reach you at your apartment. Ask you to help if you can."

"Her idea too, Johnny," Simmons said. "She was having dinner with me. Felt she ought to come along. And—"

"I'm getting out of here," Armstrong said. His heavy voice rolled over Simmons's sentence.

"I'd rather you didn't," Stein said. "Wouldn't you, Bernie?"

"Much," Bernard Simmons said and Armstrong said, "Who the hell are you?"

Simmons told the angry little man who he was.

"No affair of mine if the son of a bitch got killed," Armstrong said. "You can't make it an affair of mine. Any of you. Had a right to be here. Tell them, Meade."

"Dr. Armstrong has the use of an office here," Meade said. "To work on a book for us. For *The Guardian*."

"Until today," Armstrong said. His voice was somewhat quieter. It merely rumbled. "Got thrown out today. Didn't I, Meade? After four years of work. Tell them, Meade. Point is, isn't it—does it stick?"

"We'll talk about it," Meade said. "Monday. Perhaps—"

"No perhaps about it," Armstrong said. "It was as good as a contract."

"To me," Meade said. "I don't deny that, Cliff."

Nora could only guess what they were talking about, but felt she could guess closely enough. Lieutenant Stein, from the expression on his darkly handsome face, from the considered nodding of his head, knew precisely what they were talking about. From, Nora supposed, Meade himself.

"Dr. Armstrong," Stein said, "how long have you been here? Looking for these papers which were taken out of your office?"

"I came down here to work," Armstrong said. "Some time this afternoon. About—oh, about four, I'd say. Found I'd been evicted. And that there was a party going on. Dropped in on the party for a while. A brawl. Ask Miss Curran there."

Until he said that he had given no indication that he knew Miss Curran was there.

"After the party broke up?" Stein said and did not ask Nora anything, but looked at her and nodded his head.

"When whoever it was evicted me," Armstrong said, "they did something with a lot of notes I had. With reference books. I've been looking for them. In the offices."

"Find what you were looking for?" Stein asked him.

"No."

"Mr. Winnick had the office cleared out, Cliff," Meade said. "Probably put your papers in a storeroom. I'm sure they're safe."

"Winnick," Armstrong said. "Who the hell's Winnick? A little twerp."

Stein turned to Meade and raised black eyebrows. "Office manager," Meade told him.

"Mr. Winnick acted on instructions," Meade told the little man with the big head.

"Colley's? I'll bet they were his."

Meade did not take the bet. He did not say anything.

"Found some locked doors," Armstrong said. "Storerooms? You got keys to them, Meade?"

"No," Meade said. "Monday, Cliff."

"Then," Armstrong said, "I'm getting out of here. Whatever anybody says."

"No," Stein said. "As soon as we can manage it, Dr. Armstrong. But not yet."

Armstrong started toward the open doors to the big, desk-filled room. But Detective Paul Lane flicked a hand, the thumb up, and Patrolman O'Brien put hands back on narrow shoulders. Armstrong said several things, none of them noticeably professorial.

"Ask Dr. Armstrong to wait in one of the offices, O'Brien," Lane said. "And—wait with him."

For a moment, Armstrong twisted under the hands on his shoulders, as if he were trying to wrench himself loose. But he quit that. He said, and now spoke like a professor, "You are exceeding your authority, Lieutenant."

"If you think so," Stein said, "call your lawyer and ask him, Doctor. O'Brien will see you find a telephone and get an outside line."

O'Brien said, "Sure." Armstrong didn't say anything at all, and O'Brien turned him to face the way they had come. They walked away. After a few steps, O'Brien took his hands off the spindly man's shoulders. They kept on walking away. At the end of the corridor they turned right and disappeared.

"He's excitable, Lieutenant," Meade said. "Also, he is a very able man. In his field he is a man of considerable stature."

"We'll bear that in mind," Stein said, without inflection in his voice. "Again, Mr. Meade, I'm sorry we had to drag you away from your dinner party. And probably, when we get things straightened out a little, we'll have to ask you for help again. You'll be in town over the weekend?"

Meade nodded his head and said, "That all?" Stein said, "Certainly, Mr. Meade," and Meade said, unexpectedly, "I know you'll help the officers in any way you can, Miss Curran."

He walked away, his shoulders straight under a white dinner jacket. He walked, not into the big general room and toward the exit from it, but down the corridor, in the direction Armstrong and the patrolman had taken. Stein looked after him for a moment and then turned to Nora and shrugged his shoulders slightly and raised his eyebrows.

"He's going out what we call the 'back door,'" Nora said. "It opens off the elevator lobby. 'No Admittance' is printed on it and it's kept locked. Senior editors have keys."

Stein said, "Better put a man on it, Paul," and then "Thank you, Miss Curran. I wonder if you'd mind waiting somewhere for a few minutes? While I bring Mr. Simmons up to date?"

She said of course, and that she would be in her office, which was down that way. She pointed down the hallway. "My name's on the door," she said. "Unless they've scraped it off already."

"We'll find you," Stein said. "It shouldn't be long. Counselor?"

He turned and went into the office he had come out of—the big corner office. The door had "Jefferson Meade, Editor," lettered on it. Bernie Simmons followed him into the room and closed the door after them. As he closed it he turned and watched Nora and smiled. But he smiled only at a trim back as she walked down the corridor.

At the end of the wide hall, Nora turned right, into a somewhat narrower hallway from which, on either side, offices opened. Hers was a small, inside office—not that being on the inside of a windowless building made much difference—half way down the corridor, which ended in the back door. Nora was not one of those who had a key to it.

The door to the office opposite hers was open. It had "Rosalie Shaffner, Fashions" stenciled on the glass. Rosalie Shaffner was sitting at her desk. She had put her hair in its usual immaculate order. She had a flat attaché case on top of the desk and was taking papers out of drawers and putting them into the case. Nora looked in at her for a moment and then turned to open the door of her own office—what had been her office. On the panel of her door was stenciled, "Nora Curran, Associate." The knob made a small metallic sound as she turned it and Rosalie said, "Were you on his little list, Miss Curran?"

Nora turned and went across the hall and stood in the doorway of Rosalie's office.

"Or," Rosalie said, "if you're scouting for the management, dear—I'm taking personal things home. Leaving everything tidy for the next to come."

"I'm not scouting for anybody, Miss Shaffner," Nora said.

"Then," Rosalie Shaffner said, "happen to have a razor blade on you? I think a razor blade would do it."

"Do?"

"Scratch my name off the door," Rosalie Shaffner said. "Leave everything very tidy for the next to come."

"I'm not scouting," Nora said. "I was on the list, Miss Shaffner. And if I were scouting, it wouldn't be for Mr. Colley, would it?"

Rosalie Shaffner shook her head. Then she said, "Who else, dear? Unless, of course, that Miss Pickett?"

"Not Mr. Colley," Nora said. "Because, you see, he's dead." She paused for a moment. She said, "Hasn't anybody told you?"

Rosalie Shaffner stood up behind her desk. The movement was abrupt, almost violent. As she stood, holding to the desk, she brushed the attaché case off it. On the floor, papers fell out of the case.

She said, "What do you mean he's dead?"

"Just that," Nora said. "Somebody killed him this evening. In his office. They say with that trophy he had on it. That he won in a fishing tournament somewhere."

"My God," Rosalie Shaffner said. Then, somewhat hysterically, she laughed.

But then she sat down, as abruptly as she had stood up. She put her arms on the desk. She put her head down on her arms.

IV

The big corner office surprised Bernard Simmons when he followed Lieutenant Stein into it. Its furnishings were not, as he expected them to be—as the building itself was—stark and functional. Leather chairs and sofa; a desk with curves in it, on one side a bookcase with glass doors—all of it seemed to come from another time and another place. Behind the desk there was an oak cabinet with closed doors. There were two doors in the wall on the right as they went into the room. Two of the walls were glass, but heavy red curtains almost covered them, from ceiling down to the floor.

They sat down, neither behind the desk. They sat in deep leather chairs. The chairs were rather like those in the lounge of a club Bernard Simmons belonged to.

"Bernie," John Stein said, "is this Miss Curran at all a special friend of yours?"

Bernard Simmons had never put it quite that way to himself. He hesitated a moment and decided it was time to.

"Yes, John," he said. "We can say she is. Why? I mean, suppose she is?"

"This," Stein said. "She was apparently the last person Colley saw today. That is, the last one he fired today. He said, 'That's all, Miss Curran,' and she went out—I suppose she went out—and closed the door. Closed it rather hard."

"She's told me what he said," Simmons said. "And that she didn't say anything and went out. Under the circumstances, it would be natural for her to close the door emphatically. But how do you know about this, John?"

"Colley had a tape recorder running," Stein told him. "Damned if I know why, but he did. He fired six people this afternoon, Bernie. He was—call it abrupt, with all of them. He didn't have a nice voice, Bernie. Sounded as if he enjoyed firing people. As if—hell, as if it were some sort of a game and he was winning it. Most of the ones he fired were like Miss Curran. Didn't say much. Just accepted it. As if they'd expected it. But one of them, a"—he took a list out of his pocket and looked at it—"a Miss Shaffner. She screamed at him, Bernie. Called him, among other things, a lousy bastard. But—let's play it, shall we, Bernie? If—you still want to sit in, Bernie?"

"Yes," Simmons said. "I'll sit in, John. But before the tape, the general setup, John. What you've learned of it. From Meade. I know the United Broadcasting Network is absorbing—swallowing—*The Guardian*. Finding certain elements indigestible, evidently. And—spitting them out. And Colley was to take over for UBN?"

"For the time being, anyway," Stein said. "According to Meade. But also according to Meade, Colley wasn't actually a magazine man. At the network he's—was—something they call a program co-ordinator. They've taken over a couple of book publishing concerns recently. Each time, Colley went in and got things shaken down. And, I gathered, people shaken out. Meade—"

Jefferson Meade had not, during the half hour or so Stein had questioned him, been "forthcoming." He had been courteous and responsive. He had not volunteered information.

"Careful in what he said?"

It could be called that. Aloof might be another word for it. He had answered Stein's questions readily; he had not amplified answers. Did he know anything about Bryan Colley's personal life? "No." Was Colley well known in the field of magazine publishing? "Not primarily a magazine man." If he had lived, Colley would, for the time anyway, have run the magazine? "I would remain as editor," Meade had said to that. And now?

"That," Meade said, "is up to the board of directors. The new board. Presumably, I'll stay on as editor."

"The network will want their own man in?"

"Presumably."

"I was just scratching around, Bernie," Stein told the red-haired man. "Not knowing precisely where to scratch first. After, of course, I'd found out that Meade himself left the party early on—before seven, he says. Had a dinner engagement, went home and changed for it. Where we ran him down. He'd told his man where he'd be. Felt that the party here would get along all right without him. And he said, 'I'm getting a little old for big parties, Lieutenant.'"

"Say how old?"

Since Meade had brought the matter up, Stein had asked him about his age. Meade was sixty-four. Due to retire in another year. That he had volunteered.

He had no idea who would be sent by UBN to replace Colley. Somebody, of course, who would carry through the new plans for the magazine.

What new plans?

"I was fishing," Stein said. "Not knowing what I was fishing for precisely."

That depended on the decisions reached by the new board of directors. "Liven it up," was a term Meade had heard used. A not very specific term, obviously.

Stein had pressed a little, and got only a little. More photographs—splashing photographs apparently had helped *Craddock's Monthly*. More controversial articles. A de-emphasis on fiction. *The Guardian* had always welcomed fiction and printed a good deal of it. As the lieutenant probably knew?

"Can't remember I ever read it," Stein said to Bernie Simmons. "My wife does. Anyway, I see it around the house. I said, 'Sure,' when he asked me that. Felt he expected it. That —I don't know—that I'd have hurt his feelings if I said I didn't know anything about the magazine. By the way, he calls it 'the book.' Some people I know do too, but they're not people who read very much. Of anything."

"Hurt his feelings, Johnny?"

It was hard to put a finger on. Talking to Meade, Stein had got the impression that Meade felt that he was the magazine, not that he was merely an employee—a very senior employee, of course—of The Home Guardian Corporation. "Been with it forty years," Stein said. "He did tell me that —volunteered that. The last fifteen or so as editor."

"Resent being superseded? Apparently it more or less comes to that. Would have, anyway, with Colley on the job."

Meade had not showed resentment.

"Of course, he didn't show much of anything."

"Shock at Colley's murder? In, I gather, the room next door?"

Simmons gestured toward the doors in the wall—the wall, obviously, which separated the corner office from the office adjacent, which was the office Colley had died in.

"Said the words," Stein said. "Didn't pretend to be especially upset. Yes, Bernie. One of the doors opens into the next office. The other door's to Meade's washroom. Very complete, the washroom is. Usual things, including shower. Plus a small refrigerator, with nothing in it but ice cubes. And an electric hotplate."

Bernie Simmons considered. He put the tips of his fingers together and looked over them at Lieutenant Stein.

"Left the party before seven," Simmons said, to himself and Stein. "Go around telling people goodbye?"

"Didn't say. Didn't think to ask him. But, on the whole, I'd doubt it. Not the kind of man, at a guess, who'd make a point of leaving."

"Wouldn't myself," Simmons said. "Where does he live, Johnny?"

Meade had a house in the Sutton Place area.

"House? Then servants?"

"Housekeeper, who also cooks for him sometimes. A man, who also drives his car. Yes, Bernie. A couple of the boys have gone over." He said this last wearily. He had worked before with Bernard Simmons, and Simmons was a fine man to work with. Now and then, to be sure, he seemed to feel that policemen didn't know their business.

"Sorry, Johnny," Simmons said. "Hurt his feelings, you think, to find out he's being checked on?"

"No. Mentioned it himself. Said we'd probably want to check out on him. Said he realized we'd want to check everything we could on everybody. So—that's about it. Party was in what they call the library. All cleaned up when we got here. Maybe thirty, forty people at it. Mostly gone by seven-thirty, from what we've got so far. Out of the library, anyway. Whether they'd left the floor—*Guardian* takes the whole floor and the one below it—will take finding out. Lots of private offices they could go into, if they wanted to stick around."

"The party started?"

"Around five. After the clerical help—typists and stenographers and the like—had taken off."

"Two floors?"

"Business office on the floor below. Also the test kitchens. Sent the food for the party up from the kitchens. And, yes, Bernie. Stairway and private elevator between the two floors. Want to hear the tape now, Counselor?"

Bernie Simmons grinned at the lieutenant of detectives and, after a moment, was grinned back at. Then Bernie said, "Yes, Lieutenant."

But Detective Paul Lane knocked at the door and, without waiting for an answer, opened it. He spoke from the doorway.

"Lady just tried to leave by this back door of theirs," Lane said. "Seemed to be in rather a hurry about it. A Miss Shaffner—Rosalie Shaffner. Thought you might want to ask her what her hurry was, John."

"I'd—" Stein began and stopped. A slender woman —a youngish woman, Stein thought—jostled past Detective Lane, who drew aside to let her. He said, "Miss Shaffner, Lieutenant."

She wore a sheath dress, geometrically patterned in black and white. It fitted admirably, and she had a figure worth fitting. She said, "What on—" in a carrying voice and Stein said, "Just a moment, Miss Shaffner," and then, "Want to see how far Neely's got, Paul?"

"Transcribing," Lane said. "I'll check." He backed into the corridor and closed the door behind him.

Rosalie Shaffner had blonde hair, artfully arranged. She had grayish blue eyes, and the bones of her face were, Bernie Simmons thought, excellent. Jaw a little squared off, perhaps. In her early thirties, Bernie thought. In ten years or so, the square jaw might look like a hard jaw. Just now, a noticeably attractive woman, in a very finished way.

Both he and Lieutenant Stein had stood as Rosalie Shaffner came into the room. She looked from one to the other of them. She said, "What's this all about? And who are you two? Policemen?"

"I am," Stein said, and told her what kind of policeman. "This is Bernard Simmons," Stein said. "He's attached to the District Attorney's office. Why were you in a hurry, Miss Shaffner?"

She said she didn't know what he meant.

"Detective Lane got that impression," Stein said. "But you heard him say that, didn't you? That you were planning to leave by what is called the back door, and that you seemed to be in a hurry."

"I don't dawdle," Rosalie Shaffner said. "I never dawdle. Is it true what Nora Curran says? That somebody killed poor Bryan?"

"Yes," Stein told her. "I'm afraid somebody did."

"It's dreadful," Rosalie said. "Simply dreadful. He was a fine man, Lieutenant. A fine man and a brilliant man. It's hard to believe."

Almost everybody, Bernie thought, says that—that murder is hard to believe. You think that almost nobody read newspapers. He also thought that they had just heard the first good words anybody had spoken about Bryan Colley.

"He was a friend of yours, Miss Shaffner?" Stein said. "Sit down, won't you? We'll try not to keep you long."

"A few years ago," Rosalie said and looked around and then went to the red leather sofa and sat on it and crossed admirable legs. The sheath dress slid up them smoothly to a little above excellently articulated knees. "A few years ago I was with UBN. As a consultant. I did know Bryan then. Not terribly well. He was—he was so important, Lieutenant."

"Fashion consultant?"

"Of course. This was some time before I joined the *Guardian* staff. Actually, I hadn't seen him in ages until he came here a couple of weeks ago. To represent the network."

Stein said he saw. He said, "You were at the party this afternoon, Miss Shaffner?"

"For a little while."

"Then? I mean, you left while the party still was going on?"

She said she had. She said that she had developed a slight headache and that the party had begun to get noisy.

"When did you leave?"

She recrossed her legs and smiled gently and shook her head. The blonde hair stayed in its place. She said, "Really, Lieutenant," and there was, vaguely, pity in her voice. "I don't run on a time schedule."

"About when?"

"Does it really make any difference? Oh, probably about six-thirty."

Stein said, again, that he saw. He said, "And then?"

"Went to a quiet place I know and had a quiet dinner by myself." And then, in the same low but unexpectedly carrying, voice "And, Lieutenant, I didn't come back here after dinner and kill poor Bryan. Why ever should I?"

"No suggestion you did," Stein said. "You did come back, obviously. When, Miss Shaffner? And why?"

She looked at her watch, a small platinum lozenge on her left wrist.

Bernie looked at his own. It was a quarter after ten.

"About an hour or so ago," she said. "Went in the back door and to my office. And didn't know anything about this dreadful business until little Nora told me."

Bernie Simmons looked at Stein and raised reddish eyebrows. Stein shrugged his shoulders just perceptibly and shook his head slightly. They hadn't, Bernie gathered, got around to checking the many offices on the *Guardian* floor since they got there, which was probably about two hours ago. There had been a good many things more pressing. And there had been no reason to suppose a murderer was waiting patiently in an office to be picked up.

"My office is quite near the back door," Rosalie Shaffner said. "A long way from here. And, of course, I had my door closed."

"Why did you come back to your office?" Stein asked her.

She said, "You are nosy, aren't you?" She spoke as one who asks an unimportant but civil question.

Bernie Simmons answered the civil question. He said, "We're always nosy about murder, Miss Shaffner. Occupational routine. Why *did* you come back to your office?"

"To clear it out," Rosalie said. "Oh—you don't know, of course. I told Mr. Colley this afternoon that I was leaving. *Craddock's* has been after me for—oh, for months. And with the changes here—" She finished by shrugging shoulders slightly.

"Your decision to leave *The Guardian* was quite voluntary, Miss Shaffner? No—call it pressure?"

"Of course not. Mr. Colley urged me to stay on. At least until the next issue was put to bed. He was quite insistent, dear Bryan was. If it was a matter of money, he said, he'd take it up with Mr. Meade. As if the poor old man had any say any more. As if—"

She stopped abruptly but not, Bernie Simmons thought, as soon as she wished she had.

"I see," Stein said. "You felt that things would be different here, with the new management. And decided to accept this offer from—what was it again?"

"*Craddock's. Craddock's Monthly*. They want to replace poor dear Elaine. Everybody knows that, except, of course, Elaine herself."

"She being?" Not that it mattered to John Stein, except that he was a man who liked to clear things up as he went along.

Elaine was, for the time being, fashion editor of *Craddock's Monthly*.

"On her way out," Rosalie said, providing needless amplification. "In this business we come and go. Musical chairs, you know."

There were two quick taps on the door. Stein raised his voice a little and said, "Come in, Paul." Lane came in, carrying a couple of typed sheets.

"Just finished it, John," Lane said, and handed the sheet to Stein. Stein said, "Thanks. Found any more stragglers?"

"No," Lane said. "The professor. Who's in one of the offices, typing his head off. With O'Brien watching him. And Miss Curran, who was just sitting the last time I looked in on her. And said we were sorry to keep her waiting."

Stein nodded his head and read the typescript. He handed it to Simmons. Simmons read it more slowly and said, "Interesting, Johnny. We'd better—" He did not finish. His eyes went back to the typed sheets.

"Miss Shaffner," Stein said, "hate to keep going over things, but I wonder if you'd tell us a little more about your interview with Mr. Colley? When you told him you were leaving?"

"That was all there—" Rosalie Shaffner said, and Simmons interrupted her.

"Before you do," Simmons said, "I want to tell you this, Miss Shaffner. You don't have to tell us anything. You understand that? If you'd rather not say anything unless you have a lawyer with you, that's the way it'll be. Clear?"

"I've nothing—" she began and then fixed her eyes on the sheet of paper Simmons held. Her grayish blue eyes narrowed for a moment. She took a deep breath, high breasts rising under the figured dress. "Nothing I need a lawyer for," she said. "Have I?"

"For you to decide, Miss Shaffner," Simmons said. He handed the typed sheets back to Stein.

"It was just as I said," Rosalie Shaffner said. "I asked this Miss Pickett he brought here with him if Mr. Colley could spare me a minute. Because he seemed to have left the party. Anyway I didn't see him at it. She said she'd see and came back and said Mr. Colley wanted me to come right along. So—"

So she had gone with Miss Pickett to the office Bryan Colley was using and he had stood up behind his desk. He had said, "Yes, Miss Shaffner?"

"The 'Miss Shaffner' was because this Pickett was still there. After she went out he said—oh, I don't remember exactly. 'Sit down, Rosalie. What's on your mind?' Something like that. I told him and he tried to talk me out of it—oh, things about his counting on me to help him learn the ropes. He wasn't really a magazine man, you know. Almost all of his experience had been in broadcasting. And then what I told you about if it was a matter of money. He was—he was really very sweet about it. But I said, 'No go, Bryan. I'm sorry, but it's no go.'"

She stopped. Then she said that that was all of it. That she had gone out of Colley's office and, a little later, out of the party. And after dinner had decided to return to *The Guardian* and clear her desk.

"Why? There was some hurry about it?"

"It was—oh, I don't know, Lieutenant. I decide on something and I—I suppose I want it finished. Not dragging on. If I had waited until Monday—well, I'd have run into him again and had to go over it all again. And I'd made up my mind."

"I see," Stein said. "Will what's happened make any difference? About your leaving here, I mean?"

She didn't see why it should. Of course, if Mr. Meade turned out to be in full control again—not that she supposed he would, really—she had, after all, been on *The Guardian* a long time.

"How long, Miss Shaffner?"

"Almost three years."

Stein looked at Bernie Simmons. He said, "You want to take it, Counselor?" He held the typed sheets out to Simmons.

"It doesn't matter," Simmons said. "All right, John. You're sure you don't want to amplify anything, Miss Shaffner? Or change anything?"

"There's nothing to change," she said. "It was the way—"

She did not finish. She looked at the typed sheet Bernard Simmons was holding.

"Up to you," Simmons said. "Listen, then." He began to read:

"Woman's voice: 'Here's Miss Shaffner, Mr. Colley.' Sound of door closing. Man's voice: 'Sit down, Rosalie. Afraid I've got some bad news for you. You're through here.'

"Woman's voice, not same woman: 'Why, you—!'

" 'Nothing to do with you and me, Rosalie. Nothing personal about it. We're making some changes. Quite a few changes.'

" 'The hell it hasn't. After—only two nights ago you—butter wouldn't melt in that damn mouth of yours, would it? Nothing was going to affect me. "Not you, darling. Certainly not you." Remember?'

" 'That was two nights ago, my dear. The circumstances were different.'

" 'I'll say they were different. Did anybody ever tell you off, Bryan? Tell you what a lousy bastard you are?'

" 'No use blowing up, my dear. Thing is, you're done here. Won't fit in with the way we're going to do things.'

" 'The bright new look? The goddamn bright new look? The—what did you say the other night? About the readers we're—you said "we" then, all right—going to aim at. Something sort of funny. Wait a minute. "Beautiful girls who are happily married and have three lovely children." That was it; something like that.'

" 'Maybe I did. Nothing to do with what we've decided.'

" 'We?'

" 'Mr. Meade and I are in entire agreement. No use thinking you can go over my head.'

" 'To a figurehead. That's what it is, isn't it?'

" 'Nothing to do with you, Rosalie. Nothing here has from now on. Here.'

"Scraping sound. Could be desk drawer opening. Silence for thirty-two seconds.

"Woman's voice: 'Just like that?'

" 'Just like that. You'll find another spot. Clothes-for-the mature-woman spot. Like you've made *The Guardian* the last year or two.'

" 'Got a spot in mind, Bryan dear? Like, maybe back to the network?'

" 'No, Rosalie. That's out, I'm afraid. Nothing personal. I told you that.'

" 'Nothing to do with that hope-we'll-always-be-friends business you made noises about?'

" 'Nothing, my dear. I don't carry personal affairs into my job. No reason we shouldn't—'

"Woman's voice, very high pitched: 'You son of a bitch. You dirty lousy—'

"Pretty close to a scream, Lieutenant. Couldn't get the words. Went on for forty-five seconds. Stopped. Then Colley said, 'If you've got that out of your system, my dear, I've got other people to see.'

"Sound, probably, of a door closing. Closed hard. That's the end of that one, Lieutenant."

Simmons reached to the desk and put the typed sheets on it. He looked at Rosalie Shaffner.

She was not sitting poised on the sofa then. She was leaning forward, her hands covering her eyes.

"Well, Miss Shaffner?" Bernie Simmons said. "More like the way it was?"

She did not use words to answer. Still with her hands over her eyes, she nodded her head. It was as if her whole body nodded its admission.

"You see," Bernie said, and his voice was gentle, "Mr. Colley had a tape recorder running. Not just when he talked to you. When he fired you. When he talked to the others. Detective Neely has taken the recording down, in shorthand. And in sections. That was yours."

She did not say anything.

"You and Mr. Colley were more than the casual acquaintances you said you were, weren't you?" Stein asked her. "It sounds as if you were. Or had been until a couple of nights ago."

She sat up straight, then. Her eyes, Simmons noticed,

were entirely dry although her posture had been that of a woman crying.

"He was a louse right up to the end, wasn't he?" she said. "Getting it all on tape. Why? So he could play it over and hear how tough he was? How he was on top of everything and could make everybody squirm?"

"I don't know, Miss Shaffner," Stein said. "Perhaps it was that. Perhaps he merely wanted a record. About you and Mr. Colley?"

"That," Rosalie Shaffner said, "we'll skip, won't we? Or, maybe I'll get myself a lawyer and you can ask him questions."

"Up to you," Simmons said. "As I told you."

"One thing," she said. "On this damned tape. He talked to other people after he talked to me?"

Stein and Simmons looked at each other. It was Simmons who answered. His answer was, "Yes."

She said, "So?" and moved to stand up. She did stand up when nobody told her not to.

"Yes, Miss Shaffner," Stein said. "We've nothing more to ask you. Now, at any rate. We'll know where to reach you if there are other points we want to take up. You hadn't been planning to go away for the weekend?"

"I certainly had. Only now—"

"Yes," Simmons said. "It would be convenient for everybody if you stayed in town, Miss Shaffner. Until we get things cleared up a little."

"Otherwise?"

She started toward the door and turned and looked at them. She was as smoothly finished as she had been when she entered.

"No otherwise," Stein said. "We'd just rather you didn't go too far away."

"I could if I wanted to? You wouldn't stop me? I've heard about the material witness bit, Lieutenant."

Stein looked quickly at Bernard Simmons.

"You're quite free to go where you like, Miss Shaffner," Simmons said. "If going out of town is important to you."

"I'll think about it," Rosalie Shaffner said, and went out and closed the door firmly behind her.

Stein got up, rather quickly, and went to the door which connected the corner office with the one next it. He opened the door and said, "Miss Shaffner is leaving, Paul. Be interesting, don't you think, to know where she goes?"

"O.K.," Paul Lane said. "I'll take care of it. Miss Curran? Or the professor?"

Stein turned toward the red-haired man, who was reading the typescript. Stein said, "Hate to keep your friend hanging around, Bernie. But—"

"Oh," Bernie Simmons said. "The lady won't mind, Johnny. The eminent professor, by all means."

Stein said, "The professor, Paul. Neely got his section ready?"

Paul Lane said Neely was working on it. Stein closed the door and went back to one of the red leather chairs. Bernie Simmons still was reading from the typescript. He put it down.

"Wonder," he said, "which of them broke it off, Johnny? The pretty lady who, like the rest of us, isn't getting any younger? Or Colley, who found a girl who didn't show it yet? Put that and getting fired together, Johnny, and it might have annoyed the lady, wouldn't you think?"

V

Dr. Clifford Armstrong was not, as planned, next on the list. Lieutenant Stein and Bernie Simmons sat for some minutes waiting. Stein agreed that Miss Rosalie Shaffner might well have been annoyed if, during forty-eight hours or so, she had, involuntarily, lost both a lover and a job. He had added that there was nothing in the interview, as they heard the interview, to indicate which of the two had broken it off. If, of course, there had been anything to break off.

"I think there was, Johnny," Simmons said. "And that he was the one who did the breaking. Because, if it was the other way round, she'd have said so, I think. Made rather a point of saying so. For the most obvious reason. Humiliating to be walked out on. Perhaps for another reason. Perhaps—"

Paul Lane knocked, this time from the door to the next office, and came in. He looked rather amused.

"Our professor," Lane said, "says we kept him waiting and now we can wait. Because he's got at least another page to go. Didn't say on what. He's been pounding on a typewriter ever since O'Brien took him to the office. Hunt and peck, O'Brien says."

"He'll come when—" Stein said and then stopped, because Bernie Simmons was shaking his head.

"Order doesn't matter," he said. "Does it, Johnny? The professor is spluttery enough already. And, when we do get to him, it may take a time. Especially if he's still in a spluttering mood. Miss Curran?"

"All right," Stein said. "Paul, if you'll ask Miss Curran—"

Again he stopped and waited because, again, Simmons was shaking his head. Simmons stood up.

"All the same with you, Johnny," Simmons said, "I'll go ask the lady. Paul can tell me where she is."

"Up to you, Counselor," Stein said, and from the "Counselor" Bernie Simmons knew that Stein was a little annoyed at him—thought, as he had once or twice thought when they had worked together in the past, that Simmons was more horning in than sitting in. Which, in the past, Bernie admitted to himself, had sometimes been true enough. He had freely admitted as much to John Stein. Now he merely grinned at Stein.

"O.K., Bernie," Stein said. "Only—don't forget which side you're on."

"I never do," Simmons said, and went in the direction Paul Lane told him to take. The door to Nora Curran's office was closed and he knocked and Nora said, through the door, "Come in." When he did, she said, "Oh, it's you this time."

"Nora," Bernie Simmons said, "you told me about your interview with Colley. Just the way it happened?"

She looked surprised. Then she looked, he thought, angry. She said, "You think I lied to you, Mr. Simmons?" proving she was angry.

"Come off it, child," Bernie said, letting patience sound in his voice. "Of course I don't think you've lied to me. Point is, anybody's memory can be tricky. You're pretty sure you didn't forget anything?"

"Like hitting Colley over the head with a bronze statue?"

Bernie produced a long sigh of resignation.

"Not the sort of thing I'd be likely to forget, Bernie," Nora said. Then she said, "Oh, all right. I told you what I remembered. It was a short interview. I don't think I forgot anything. I don't say it was verbatim. Does it matter?"

"Only," Bernie Simmons said, "that Colley had a tape recorder running. God knows why. Perhaps he wanted to prove to his board of directors what an efficient operator he was. Anyway—Stein likes to have things match."

"They'll match," Nora said. "If nobody's tampered with the recording. Time for the third degree, Bernie?"

"Johnny Stein likes to hear things first hand," Simmons

said. "It's his investigation. And, Miss Shaffner says she first heard from you that Colley had been killed."

"She was in her office with the door open and—"

"No point in telling it twice, dear," Bernie said.

She had been sitting at her desk. She stood up.

"Nora," Simmons said, "when this—when this thing happened to your sister, was there any publicity? In the papers?"

"A paragraph in the *Times*," Nora said. "It didn't give Dorothy's name. Just the name of the girl who stopped her from jumping. But there was more in the *Daily News*. Girl saves roommate at risk of her own life. That sort of thing. In exclusive women's college. The story did use Dorothy's name. Why, Bernie?"

But before he could answer she said, "Oh. Because it can be followed up? Until the police find out how badly I need money just now? And hence a job? You want me to tell them about that, Bernie? But—I've already told you, haven't I? And —you're the police too, aren't you? Come down to it, aren't you?"

"In a way, I suppose so."

"I thought," Nora Curran said, "that I was telling my troubles to a friend, you know. Crying on a friend's shoulder."

"A friend," Bernie said. "At least a friend, dear."

"Whose side are you on?" she asked him, and the question echoed. It also disturbed.

"There isn't any difference between the sides," Bernie said. "If I were you, I wouldn't keep anything back. I know it's not pertinent. And—as long as I know that, my dear, I'll leave it up to you what you tell Stein."

"You're—what's the term? Officer of something—"

"Officer of the court," Bernie told her. "For some years, Nora. And I've learned to decide what I think is pertinent and what isn't. Let's go talk to Johnny."

But, back in the corner office, they did not immediately talk to Lieutenant John Stein, Homicide North. Stein was sitting at Meade's desk and he stood up when they went into the office and said, "Sorry to have kept you waiting, Miss Curran.

Only a couple of questions, probably. But first, something I want you to listen to."

A tape recorder was on the desk. He moved a switch. The playback was amplified.

There was a sound of a door opening; there was "Here's Miss Curran, Mr. Colley." There was "Sit down, Miss—" and a pause and, faintly, the rustle of paper. Then—"Curran."

The tape recording ran on for several minutes. Bernie Simmons was not surprised, but he was pleased. Nora was a good girl with a good memory. She had come as close as made no difference to the verbatim she had hesitated to promise.

The last taped words were, "That's all, Miss Curran."

There was the sound of a door closing. It sounded firmly closed, but not slammed. Stein reached toward the switch, but did not press it. There was, for some seconds, only the tape's own surface sound. Then there was the sound of a cough, brief and dry. Stein's finger was on the switch, but he did not press it.

For perhaps thirty seconds there was again only the machine's whirring. Then there was the click a door latch makes when a knob is turned, and, faintly, a grating sound. Then the recording stopped.

"Miss Curran," Stein said, "when you left Mr. Colley's office. Went out into the corridor. Was there anybody in it? Say, waiting in it? To go into Mr. Colley's office? This Miss Pickett? Anyone?"

"No. I didn't see anyone. I—I just walked down the corridor and out the back door. You don't need a key to get out that way. Only to get in."

"You didn't go back into Colley's office—the office next door to this one—after you left it?"

"I heard the door latch. On the tape, I mean. No, Lieutenant. I didn't go back in and kill Mr. Colley with that—that silly trophy on his desk."

"Take it easy, Miss Curran," Stein said. "Somebody, from the sound, did open the door. Presumably opened the door to go into the office. If there wasn't anybody in the hallway—"

"No, Johnny," Simmons said. "You're jumping, I think. Somebody opened a door. It may have been Colley himself, going out. Or—there are two doors to the office, Johnny. One opens into this office. Colley may have come in here to go to the john. Or to make himself a drink."

"To me," Stein said, "it sounded like the door Miss Curran closed when she went out. From the—oh, I don't know. The placing of the sound. But, I suppose you're right, Counselor. Miss Curran, about when did Miss Pickett ask you to go to Colley's office? I suppose that was the way it was?"

"Yes. I was summoned. At about seven."

"We know how long you were there. Ten minutes at the outside. We'll time it, of course, but about that. Then you went out of Colley's office and out the back door."

"I stopped at my office for a moment. I'd—I'd typed out a draft of a letter. I wanted it. Then—oh, yes, I went to the women's room. The powder room. Then I went out the back door and walked to my apartment."

"Walked? It was a hot evening for walking."

"It isn't far. And there weren't any cabs."

"Walked home," Stein said. "Got there about—"

"About twenty-five after seven," Bernie Simmons said. "I was propping up the wall outside her apartment. We went in and had a drink. And she told me she'd been fired. And we went out to dinner and were just finishing it when you called, Johnny. Then we came here."

Stein, still sitting behind the desk, nodded his head. He said, "Miss Curran, we were talking to Miss Shaffner a few minutes ago. She said it was you who told her Mr. Colley had been killed. That she hadn't known it until you told her. Mind telling us about that, Miss Curran?"

She told him about that.

"She seemed surprised?"

"Yes. I don't think she—" She stopped. "She seemed surprised," she said. "I'm sure she was. And—shocked. Really shocked."

"First she laughed," Stein said. "Hysterically, would you say?"

"It must have been that. Because, as I just told you, she put her head down on her arms as—as if she had almost been knocked down by it. So I—I didn't want to stand there looking at her. I went across the hall to my office."

"She was packing up to leave, you say. Did you think, from the way she acted, she'd been fired? Or had left the job voluntarily?"

"At first," Nora said, "I assumed she'd been on Mr. Colley's list. But then—it wasn't clear, Lieutenant. There was a rumor a few weeks back that *Craddock's* was after her. She never confirmed it herself. There are a lot of rumors in our business."

"Lot of rumors everywhere," Stein said. "Were there rumors before today the new management was going to let some of the staff go?"

"Yes. There was guessing as to who."

"Did you expect to be one of those let go, Miss Curran?"

She thought about that. She was sitting erect on the sofa, her knees and feet together. Doesn't fidget, Bernie Simmons thought, approving.

"No," Nora said. "I didn't, really. I thought—I was afraid —that Mr. Simpson would be fired. It was common guessing the UBN wanted to make *The Guardian* more like *Craddock's Monthly*. Which would have meant less fiction. A lot less."

"If he'd gone and you'd stayed on would you have taken over the fiction editorship? I mean, had that occurred to you?"

"You wouldn't believe me if I said it hadn't, would you, Lieutenant? Or that I like Kent Simpson—and think that he's a hundred times as good at the job as I ever would have been?"

Her face changed a little, Bernie thought, with the change of tense. Only a little. Not that Johnny Stein wouldn't notice even a little.

"A disappointment, then," Stein said. "Even something of a shock, Miss Curran?"

"It's always a shock to lose a job. Particularly—"

She broke off and looked at Bernie Simmons and she smiled and nodded her head and then she said, "Yes, Bernie." She turned back to Lieutenant Stein.

"Particularly just now," she said. "Mr. Simmons thinks I ought to tell you. Because, I guess, he thinks you'd find out anyway. And—I've rather put you on the hook, haven't I, Bernie?"

"No," Bernie Simmons said. "But I think you're right, Nora."

"I've a much younger sister," Nora said. "I just agreed—"

She told him about Dorothy and about what Dr. Werkes had advised. Stein listened, his dark face grave. There was, Bernie Simmons thought of the man he knew well, sympathy in the tall detective's dark eyes.

"I'm sorry about your sister, Miss Curran," Stein said, when she had finished. "It's a bad thing to happen. I'm sorry that this has had to come up top of it." He turned to the red-haired man. "I don't think we need to bother Miss Curran any more tonight," he said. "Do you, Bernie?"

"Miss Curran has been most helpful," Bernie Simmons said, using staid words but with great lightness in his voice. "And I think that, unless you want to go ahead with it by yourself, we'll let the professor wait a bit longer while I take Miss Curran home."

"I can perfectly well—" Nora said and Simmons said, "Come off it, dear."

She came off it and thought how much Bernie's face brightened when he was pleased.

A police sedan took them from the *Guardian* building to her apartment. While the car waited, he went up to her floor with her and down the hallway to the door of her apartment. He kissed her there, more closely than they had kissed before.

"You're a good girl, Nora Curran," Bernie said. "A very good girl. The best of all possible girls, darling."

Then he went back down to the waiting car and back to the bright coolness of the thirty-seventh floor of the *Guardian* building. Stein had waited to call Dr. Clifford Armstrong in to explain himself.

Detective Paul Lane was asked to get Dr. Clifford Armstrong, whether he had finished his page or not. And whether he was spluttery or not.

"Get Miss Curran home all right?" Stein said, as a formality. Bernie Simmons said he had got Miss Curran home all right.

"Bad thing about her sister," Stein said. "She's very fond of her sister, isn't she, Bernie?"

"Yes. Dorothy's the only family she has."

"Tough," Stein said. "Very tough. Learns—last night, wasn't it?—that her kid sister's best chance, maybe her only chance to come out of it, is to go to a private sanitarium. Today, gets fired. When she didn't expect it."

"Yes," Bernie said. "She's had a bad twenty-four hours or so. Where's our ruffled professor?"

"He'll be along," Stein said. "Since you weren't here I told Paul not to hurry him. Private sanitariums cost a lot of money, Bernie. Happen to know whether your friend Miss Curran has a lot of money?"

"She hasn't. And I'm ahead of you, Johnny. And killing Colley wouldn't get her job back. Wouldn't, as far as I can see, get any of their jobs back. I doubt if any of them thought it would, Johnny."

John Stein looked thoughtfully at Simmons for some seconds. Then he said he wasn't so sure.

"While you were taking Miss Curran home," Stein said, "I listened to the tape again. Particulary to the talk Colley had with a man named Stubbs. Had more to say than most of the others, Stubbs did. Rather interesting, Stubbs was. Lives over in Plainfield, New Jersey. There now. I've asked him to come in and he's cooperative."

"Stubbs?"

"Advertising manager. Until today, that is. Fairly big shots advertising managers are, I take it."

"Booted too?"

"Yes. Only he seems to think he can go over—"

Paul Lane opened the door. He reached around Clifford Armstrong to do it. Armstrong shook his big head.

"I've decided," he said, "that I don't want to talk to you, Lieutenant. Or to you, whoever you are. Clerk from the district attorney's office?"

"Not precisely," Simmons said. "And it's perfectly true you don't have to talk to us, Professor Armstrong. Your attorney will tell you that. Or have you already talked to him?"

"I haven't got a lawyer," Armstrong said. "What would I need a lawyer for?"

"Advice," Simmons told him. "He'd advise you, for one thing, that you can be held as a material witness."

"Only," Armstrong said, "I didn't witness anything. Or know anything about Colley's killing. Wasn't anywhere near the office they say somebody killed him in."

John Stein shook his head sadly. There was an implication of a "tut-tut" in the shaking of his head, although he did not make that sound.

"I'm afraid that isn't true, Dr. Armstrong," was what he did say. He said it with apparent sorrow. Then he said, "Perhaps you're right, Bernie. Perhaps we'd better book the professor as a material witness. And be sure he doesn't say anything more until he's got a lawyer with him."

"Probably best," Bernie said, in much the same sorrowful tone. "Don't want to deny him any of his rights. Right not to talk. If, of course, he feels talking would tend to incriminate him."

"I," Armstrong said, "have got a wife and three children. You can't lock me up. They need me."

"Oh," Simmons said, "people held as material witnesses can get bail, Professor. Wouldn't be locked up more than a day or two, probably. Perhaps just overnight, if you've got a good lawyer."

Armstrong walked over to one of the red leather chairs and sat in it.

"I," he said, "am staying right here."

"No," Stein said, "I'm afraid not, Professor. You see, Mr. Simmons and I have a good many things to do. People to talk to—people who are willing to cooperate with us. Help us find out who killed Mr. Colley. Not people who start out by lying to us."

"I didn't—"

"Yes," Stein said. "You said, just a moment ago, that you

hadn't been anywhere near the office Mr. Colley was killed in. You were, Professor. And you were told that *The Guardian*, which seemed to have become Mr. Colley, had decided it didn't want this book you've been working on. And, it seems, getting advances on."

"And where," Armstrong said, "did you get that crazy idea, Lieutenant? It was Mr. Meade ordered the book, not this man Colley. Why would I talk to Colley about it?"

Stein sighed and shook his head and looked at Bernie Simmons, who sighed and shook his head. They were both, very evidently, disappointed in Dr. Clifford Armstrong.

"If," Armstrong said, "somebody told you Colley and I had a conference about 'We, the Inheritors,' somebody lied to you. Somebody—"

"Listen, Professor," Stein said, and touched the switch of the recorder on the desk. It whirred for a moment, making a slithering sound. Then a woman's voice came on and the woman said, "Here's Professor Armstrong, Mr. Colley," and a man said, "Come in and sit down, Professor. This won't take long."

"I don't know who the hell you are," a man said, and the heavy voice was unmistakably that of the man with a big head, who had now turned to face the box on the desk.

"Let me introduce myself." The tone was ironic. "Bryan Colley. Representing the new management here, Professor. Hadn't you heard about it?"

"All I know is, some high-handed bastard cleared everything out of my office. Was that your bright idea, Colley? *Mister* Colley?"

"I had it done. You won't be needing the office any more, Professor. Your notes and other papers are quite safe. Winnick will give them to you Monday."

"What's the matter with now?"

"Mr. Winnick has other things to do just now. Monday will do, since there's no rush about anything, Professor. Because, you see, *The Guardian* has decided it doesn't want your book. Didn't work out as Mr. Meade thought it would."

"And that's a lie. Meade's seen damn near half of it. And

it's just what he had in mind and I've got a letter from him says so. It's—what the hell's going on here, Colley? It's with the stuff somebody stole out of my desk."

"I don't know what Mr. Meade may have told you, Professor. I've read part of what you showed him. As much of it as I could manage. It's very dull, Professor—dull and ponderous and nothing *The Guardian* would consider printing. I doubt very much if anybody will, Professor. In short, it's drivel. Academic drivel."

"Why, you—you—"

"Sit down, Professor."

"And who are you, you bastard? What do you know about it? About anything? Some sort of TV hack, aren't you? Remember a special you people did? Some junky title—wait a minute. *That Was Day Before Yesterday*. Remember that? It had your name on it. Associate producer, or something like that. Remember now, Colley?"

"Vaguely. It was several years ago. Hasn't anything to do with what we're talking about."

"You think I didn't know my own material when I heard it? Garbled. Out of context. But mine all the same. Because, Colley, I did a lot of research on the period and used the material in *Mores of the Mid-Nineteenth Century*. And a lot you people used and garbled wasn't anywhere else than in my book. Which wasn't mentioned, was it? So you just stole it, didn't you?"

"Apparently the network's lawyers didn't think so, Professor. And, speaking of money—of stealing, if you like—the payments *The Guardian* has made you over the last several years were made contingent on your submission of an acceptable manuscript. Which you didn't do. So—"

"And that's another of your lies. And it's one Meade won't go along with. I suppose the next thing you'll say is *The Guardian* wants the money back. That it, you squirt?"

"Sit down, Armstrong. And take your pudgy little hand off that. The rod's sharp. Might cut you."

There was a sound which might have been that of a chair pushed back. Then, very harshly, "Sit down. Sit down and shrink your head. God knows it needs shrinking. I said, *sit down!*"

There was a pause and then, from Colley, "That's better. Yes, we do want the money back, Armstrong. Because you didn't fulfill your part of the agreement. Turned in part of a lousy book. Which has cost *The Guardian* around twenty thousand."

"Meade won't have any part of that. Meade's an honest, decent man, you—"

Armstrong's voice went on for some seconds. There was turbulence in the heavy voice; it was like surf beating. The surf of the voice beat down some of the words the professor used to describe Bryan Colley. They were not professorial words. After almost a minute, Colley's sharp, hard voice cut through the rumble.

"Shut up," Colley said. "And get out. And dig up the money you owe us."

Armstrong did not immediately shut up. But the rumble receded and then there was the sound of a door opening and then of a door slamming.

There was the rustling of papers for a second or two. Then there was, faintly, the sound of a buzzer.

Lieutenant Stein switched the recorder off.

"What was it Colley told you to take your hand off of, Professor?" Stein said. "That fishing trophy he had on his desk? The statue—the heavy bronze statue—of a fisherman holding a rod out in front of him."

"I don't remember. I—I was sore. I stood up. I don't know why, exactly. I may have grabbed hold of his desk to pull myself up. Maybe one of my hands hit that damn thing."

"Colley was quite right about the rod's being sharp, Professor. Not really pointed, but sharp enough. With the weight of the statue behind it. The rod went through the corner of Colley's right eye, Professor. And into Colley's brain."

Professor Armstrong stood up.

"Assuming," he said, "Colley had one. I didn't perform the no doubt interesting experiment. I have the greatest respect for whoever did. So now?"

"What did you do after you left Colley's office?"

"Found the office of this man Winnick. Hell of a lot of offices in this place. Went into all the wrong ones first."

"Eventually, you found Winnick's office. And?"

"Tried to find his keys. Found some—quite a lot. Nothing to show what locks they opened. So I went around trying to find out."

"Looking for your papers? And, particularly, for this letter you say Mr. Meade wrote you, saying he liked the part of your book he'd read?"

"Yes."

"Find what you were looking for?"

"No. So, now?"

Stein looked at Bernie Simmons and said, "Anything you'd like to ask the professor, Counselor?"

"You've covered the ground, Lieutenant," Simmons said. "For now. We'll probably want to talk to the professor again. When we're a little further along. But as for now—" He shrugged his shoulders.

"We've got your address, Professor?"

"That man in there," Armstrong said, and jerked his right thumb toward the door between the offices.

His hands weren't really especially pudgy, Bernie Simmons thought.

VI

When the telephone rang she thought at first she would not answer it. She thought, I've had it; utterly had it. I can't take anything else. I want only to hide in myself.

For half an hour after Bernie Simmons had taken her to the door and kissed her and told her something—oh yes, that she was the best of all possible girls—she had sat quietly, hiding inside herself. She felt, sitting so, waiting for the air conditioner to catch up with the heat in the apartment, a kind of hopelessness. She felt that any movement, or any thought, would be insurmountably difficult. Even undressing and going to bed seemed something impossible to do. As for answering the telephone—

Then it was as if fingers snapped in her mind—snapped her out of hiding. It might be Dr. Werkes calling to tell her something about Dorothy. It might be Bernie, to tell her something about murder—to tell her that the good words he had promised to speak for her hadn't been good enough.

She had to cross the room to get to the telephone. It was a long way across the room. She said, "Hello," and then, because her voice was so muted to her own ears, she again said, "Hello?"

"Miss Curran? I hope I'm not calling too late?"

It was a man who hoped he was not too late. She did not recognize the man's voice.

"Jefferson Meade," the man said. "I hope I didn't waken you?"

She said, "No, Mr. Meade. You didn't waken me."

"I know it's late," Meade said. "But I wonder if I could send the car over for you? I'd like to talk to you. I've something to tell you. Ask you, rather. About *The Guardian.* Something I'd like to get settled tonight."

"Why—"

"I'd very much appreciate your coming. I can't very well leave here. I'm expecting a call. Several calls, as a matter of fact. And—I hope I have good news for you, Miss Curran. May I send the car?"

She said, "Yes, Mr. Meade. Of course."

"Shouldn't be more than ten minutes," Meade said, and hung up.

She sat at the telephone table. She was not hiding any more. But she was puzzled, and, dimly, doubtful and disturbed. It had been Mr. Meade. Of course it had been Mr. Meade. But what could he have to tell her, the smallest of small fry? Now, on *The Guardian,* not even that any more. Unless—

She groped for something tangible. She came up with nothing. Conceivably, what Meade had to tell her was that she wasn't fired any more. But that would not require an interview; that would require only a few words. "You're back on the staff, Miss Curran." And the answer would be as brief— "I'm glad, Mr. Meade."

A hoax of some sort? But that was meaningless. You're inventing complications, she told herself. Half inventing them. Mr. Meade wants to see you about something and something which has to do with *The Guardian.* So, you are not, finally, off the *Guardian* staff. That is logical. That is the only thing that is logical. She went to a window from which she could look down on the street five floors below. She stood there, looking—watching cabs go by and private cars go by. After five minutes or so a big car pulled up in front of the apartment building and stopped and a man in uniform got out of it and walked across the sidewalk toward the building. In a minute or two the house telephone buzzed and she went to it and said, "Yes?"

"Car for you, Miss Curran," Fred said from the lobby.

For a moment she hesitated, her mind fuzzy with doubt. But then she said, "I'll be right down, Fred," and got her handbag and took seconds to check her face in a compact's mirror. Then she went down.

The chauffeur was reassuring—an elderly, substantial man in uniform. A solid man. The car was reassuring. It was a Cadillac of dignity. The chauffeur held the door open for her and she got into the car. There was nobody waiting for her in the back seat. It had been ridiculous, melodramatically ridiculous, to have momentarily wondered whether there might be.

The big car went east, then up town and then east again. It stopped in front of a narrow house and the chauffeur opened the car door for her and, when she had gone up three steps to the door of the house, said, "Let me, miss," and reached ahead of her and opened the door. She went in and the chauffeur went in after her and said, "Mr. Meade's in the drawing room, miss. On your right." He gestured toward her right.

Meade, still in a white dinner jacket, met her at the door and held a hand out to her and told her it was good of her to come.

The room was high-ceilinged. It was long and narrow as the house was narrow. The room was pleasantly cool.

"I do hope," Jefferson Meade said, "that I didn't waken you, Miss Curran. I do realize that you must have had a trying day, as we all have. Perhaps a drink?"

She said she didn't think so.

"I hope," Meade said, "—sit down, Miss Curran—I hope the police didn't give you a bad time."

She sat down in the chair he gestured toward. She said, "Asked me about being called into Mr. Colley's office this afternoon. And being told my services wouldn't be required any more. You knew he fired several people today, Mr. Meade? At the party?"

"Oh, yes," Meade said, and sat down in a facing chair. "That is, I knew he was going to. And, regretted that the new management found it necessary. I was powerless to prevent it, Miss Curran. They went over my head, as the saying is."

She merely nodded her head to that.

"Mr. Colley's death has changed things," Meade said.

"Surprisingly. UBN has decided not to replace Colley, at least for the time being. For the time being they're—they're going to let us jog along in our old-fashioned way. Under my old-fashioned editorship. I'm not at all clear why. Why Colley's death should change things. Does cigar smoke bother you?" He reached to the table beside his chair and opened a humidor and looked at her. He raised heavy white eyebrows. She said, "Not at all, Mr. Meade," and he took a long cigar out of the humidor and clipped it with silver clippers and lighted it, unexpectedly with a match.

"But," Meade said, "Colley's death *has*, temporarily, altered policy. Only temporarily, of course. But, meanwhile, for as long as we jog along, would you like to be fiction editor, Miss Curran?"

She repeated, "Fiction editor?" which was a meaningless thing to do. Momentarily, it was as if her mind were sheathed, filmed off from the reality of words—even of words as clearly spoken as Meade's had been. When she did speak, it was slowly, ploddingly.

"Kent is fiction editor," she told the man who had made Kent Simpson that. "Mr. Simpson. If things are going on for now as they were before, Mr. Simpson will be fiction editor. Unless—"

She stopped and the film vanished from around her mind.

"He's very good, Mr. Meade," she said. "He's one of the best."

"My dear Miss Curran," Meade said, "I know quite well that Kent Simpson is good. You won't be taking his job away from him. Actually, it was he who suggested I talk to you."

She shook her head.

"As soon as this man from the network—executive vice-president he is; man named Cooper—asked me to carry on for the time being and I had said I would, I began calling people up. People Colley fired today; began trying to pull the staff back together. Some of them I couldn't get—Miss Shaffner, for example, didn't answer the phone. I did get Kent Simpson."

And, Meade told Nora Curran, Kent Simpson said he didn't want the job back. "Being sacked," Simpson said—Meade told Nora Simpson had said—"made up my mind for me. Or, brought forward in my mind what had been in the back of it for a year or two."

What had been in the back of Simpson's mind, waiting to be pushed forward in it, was the decision to get back to his own work, which was writing stories, not deciding to accept or reject other people's stories. His wife had been wanting him to do that. "Not live any more at the mercy of the New Haven," Simpson told Meade from New Canaan, amusement in his voice. Flora Simpson had also told her husband that he was a writer, and that the job of a writer is to write. Full time.

"I've been working on a novel for a couple of years," Simpson told Meade. "Nights and weekends. Showed about a third of it to a publisher. And, believe it or not, got an advance. So, Jeff, I guess I'll just stay fired. If it's all right with you and UBN. Or, I guess, even if it isn't. Because, with my wife and me, it suddenly turns out to be just dandy."

Jefferson Meade drew on his cigar and turned so that he did not exhale the smoke directly at Nora Curran. But it floated between them. There was, she thought, looking at him through the moving smoke, amusement in his lean brown face.

"Actually," Meade said, "I think he and Flora had had an extra drink or two to celebrate his getting fired. I really think they had, Miss Curran. So—Monday we confer about what's in the fiction bank? A one-shot for the A issue is set, isn't it?"

"Yes. And two of the shorts. The short bank is rather low, Mr. Meade. A good many of the people who used to be regulars—well, they're not sending much in any more."

"When a writer had half a dozen markets it was one thing," Meade said. "With only a couple, a pro turns to something else. Understandably. So—you're fiction editor for now, Miss Curran. What have we been paying you?"

She told him.

"We can up that a bit," he said. Then he looked at her intently. He said, "Are you all right, Miss Curran?"

"Knocked over, actually," she said. "Even good news can knock you over, Mr. Meade."

"Good news should be celebrated," Meade said, and reached to the table which held the humidor and pressed a button inlaid in it. And almost at once the man who had driven her there came in from the rear of the long cool room. He had a white jacket on this time and he said, "Sir?"

"Scotch mist," Meade said. "And—Miss Curran?"

She started again to refuse a drink but thought, he will misunderstand, and said, "Could I have a very light Scotch and plain water?"

The chauffeur-houseman said, "Certainly, Miss Curran," and went back down the long room.

"Good," Meade said. "It's been quite a day, hasn't it? Tell me, Miss Curran, was Colley rude to you?"

"Abrupt," she said. "As if—oh, as if I were an object. He couldn't remember my name. Or pretended he couldn't."

"He was an odd man," Meade said. "I thought that from what I'd heard before he—moved in on us. More after I'd met him. Very efficient, of course. But not a magazine man. Thank you, Alfred."

The houseman put glasses down. He said, "Thank you, sir. Miss." He went back the way he had come.

"Not an endearing man, Colley," Meade said. "Nevertheless, murder is incomprehensible, isn't it? To a—call it an outsider. I suppose it isn't, isn't at all, to men like this Lieutenant Stein. Or, of course, men like your red-haired friend. The— it is assistant district attorney, isn't it?"

"Attached to the District Attorney's Homicide Bureau," she told him. "Actually, assistant bureau chief. Or, I think the term is deputy bureau chief. His name is Bernard Simmons, Mr. Meade."

"Seems capable," Meade said. "So does the police lieutenant, of course. I suppose they'll make even a thing like this comprehensible. Perhaps they already have."

She did not know. She thought that, at least when they finished with her, they seemed still in the middle of things.

"They seemed," Nora said, "to be concentrating on the people who were on Mr. Colley's list. His firing list. I suppose they think that one of—one of us—blew up after he was dismissed. Went back and grabbed whatever was nearest and hit Mr. Colley in the head with it. But I don't know what they think, Mr. Meade."

"The way Mr. Simmons's mind works?" Meade said. It was only half a question. She answered it with a shake of her head. She sipped from her glass; it was good Scotch. She reached down to the handbag on the floor beside her chair and opened the bag and groped in it.

"A cigarette?" Meade said, and got up and took an engraved wooden box the few steps to her chair and opened the box. She took a cigarette out of it. The cigarette had the initials "J. M." on it. He lighted the cigarette, again with a match, and went back to his own chair.

"Not," Nora said, "in things like this. Not the way his mind works professionally. We're just friends. He takes me to dinner and we go dancing sometimes. We don't talk about his cases. I suppose he's not supposed to."

"And," Meade said, "I don't doubt you two have better things to talk about, Miss Curran. You think they're concentrating on the people Mr. Colley decided to let go? You among them, of course."

"I was the last one he interviewed, apparently," she said. "If you could call it interviewing. The last one to see him alive. Except the one who killed him. They asked me about what he said and I told them and, fortunately, I'd remembered it right. Anyway, it matched the recording."

He said, "Recording? What recording, Miss Curran?"

It seemed, she told him, that Bryan Colley had had a tape recorder running while he was telling members of the staff, starting with Kent Simpson, that they were no longer members of the staff. She knew that Simpson had been one of those fired. She thought Rosalie Shaffner had been another.

"Yes," Meade said. "Simpson and Miss Shaffner and poor Fremont and Stubbs. Although Stubbs has a contract and will have to be paid off. And he told Cliff Armstrong we weren't going to use the long article—really a book—he'd been working on. I objected to that, and was overruled."

He shook his head slowly.

"Strange to be overruled in my own shop," Jefferson Meade said. He drank from his glass. "Very strange," he said. "To be told, in effect, that I was to stay on as a figurehead. Until retirement time came up. However—" He shrugged his shoulders and again raised his glass. He said, "Why on earth should he want that kind of recording?"

"I don't know, Mr. Meade," Nora said. "Perhaps to prove to somebody he'd done his job?"

"Perhaps just to play it back and—and listen to people squirm," Meade said. "He was rather like that, perhaps. And—very dominating. I'd only known him for three weeks or so. Actually known him. I may be unfair. And I can't, obviously, claim to be impartial. I don't like to see *The Guardian* changed. Made another *Craddock's Monthly*." Again he shrugged his shoulders. Then he emptied his glass. He looked at Nora's, which was more than half full. She shook her head. Meade reached again to the button inlaid in the table by his chair. When the houseman appeared at the end of the long room, Meade said, "You're sure, Miss Curran?" and, when she said she was quite sure, Meade raised his own glass in signal.

"I gather," Meade said, "that the recorder wasn't running when—when poor Colley actually was killed. No—oh, sound of a blow? Suitable, 'Don't! *Don't!*' Followed by a name?"

"As far as I know," she said, "the recording stopped with me. At least, it seemed to. They may merely have cut it off there, but I think it was turned off. I suppose by Mr. Colley."

"How did it end?" Meade asked her. Then he shook his head, she thought at himself, in deprecation of himself. He said, "We all like to play detective, I suppose. Although, under these circumstances, it's a strange part to play."

"It ended," she said, "my part of it ended, with the sound of my closing the door when I went out of the office. At least

—no, wait. There was another sound, after a few seconds. The sound, I thought—and Bernie and Lieutenant Stein seemed to think—of the door being opened again."

"The same door? The one into the corridor?"

"It sounded the same to me, Mr. Meade. And to Lieutenant Stein. Bernie—Mr. Simmons—did say something about there being a second door. The one into the next office."

"Yes," Meade said. "*My* office."

He put the full glass the houseman had brought him down hard on the table. He said, "My God," and then, for no reason she could think of, "Sorry, Miss Curran. It does raise an unpleasant possibility. That somebody was using my office to hide in. While he waited until it was time to kill."

"Bernie was only—guessing, Mr. Meade," Nora said. "Raising a possibility. To me, and to the lieutenant, it sounded like the same door. The one I went out of. Only—" She stopped. After a second he said, "Only?"

"The sound of the door opening," she said, "was only seconds after the sound of the door—the door I used—closing. But when I went out there wasn't anybody in the corridor. Anybody waiting to go in."

"While you were with Mr. Colley," Meade said, "you didn't hear any sound from my office? Something, say, that the recorder wouldn't pick up? The sound of somebody moving?"

"I don't remember anything. I—I was listening to Mr. Colley. Hearing myself fired. At a bad time for me. An especially bad time."

He merely raised his eyebrows.

"A family obligation," she said. "It—it doesn't matter. Particularly now that I've got this—this reprieve."

"I hope," Meade said, "that it may turn out to be more than that, Miss Curran. Are you sure you won't let Alfred freshen your drink?"

She was still quite sure. She was also sure that Jefferson Meade could see that her glass was still half full. She moved forward in her chair and, when he did not protest, stood up. He stood too.

"I do appreciate this chance," she said. "It's—it's something I never thought possible. I hope I'll be up to it, Mr. Meade."

"Haven't any doubt of that," Meade said and pressed the table button once more. This time when the houseman came he was a chauffeur again.

VII

H. R. Stubbs was not tall but he was noticeably erect. He had brown, brush-cut hair and his shoulders were square under the jacket of an Italian silk summer suit which his drive in from Plainfield had neither dampened nor wrinkled. Air-conditioned car, Bernie Simmons guessed; probably air-conditioned house in Plainfield. Mr. Stubbs had the appearance of a man who would immunize himself against summer's heat, except when on the golf course. Or, more likely, Simmons thought, the tennis court. Stubbs was a wiry man, still young enough for tennis

Stubbs quite understood that the police had to interview anybody who might throw light on this tragic occurrence. There was no reason, none whatever, why they should apologize for dragging him in from Plainfield. (The "apology" had been Stein's, "Sorry we had to put you to this trouble, Mr. Stubbs.") Stubbs wanted very much to help, as he was sure everybody did. He was afraid he could tell them little that might help. But anything he could do—

"We're talking to everybody who saw Mr. Colley this afternoon," Stein said. "As a formality, Mr. Stubbs. A place to start. I gather you were one of those who talked to him? Do you mind telling us about it?"

"Why should I, Lieutenant? Colley asked me to come to his office." He identified the adjacent office with a gesture. "He told me that UBN, now it had acquired a controlling interest, was making certain changes. And that I was one of the changes. That is, of course, that the position of advertising manager was one of the changes. In short, that I was out."

"And you?"

"Told him I had a contract with more than a year to run. That UBN could pay up on it or its lawyers and my lawyers could fight it out. The whole of it took about three minutes."

"How did he take it?"

"Said, we'd see about that, and I said we sure as hell would see about that. And left."

"That was all? There wasn't anything more?"

"Why should there have been? New management or not, Bryan Colley or not, *The Guardian* has a legal obligation. There aren't any loopholes. I've got a good lawyer."

"That was all you said to Colley?"

"I may have said one or two other things. That was the gist of it."

"For example, Mr. Stubbs? I may as well tell you that Colley had a tape recorder running while you talked to him. While all the others talked to him. You knew he fired several members of the editorial staff this afternoon, Mr. Stubbs?"

"No. But I'm not surprised. 'Clean-sweep Colley,' they call him. The man with the new broom. And, a man to ride high on it while he had it."

"While he had it," Stein repeated. "Was that what you meant when you said—" He looked at a typewritten sheet in front of him. "When you said, 'It's fifty-fifty, Colley, that you're sticking your neck out. A long way out. That the chances are at least even they'll pull the rug out from under you.' Is that what you meant?"

"Mixed metaphors a bit, didn't I?" Stubbs said. "Yes. He was on a spot, actually. And, of course, knew it. That it was entirely probable that some of them were giving him enough rope."

" 'They'll pull the rug out,' " Stein said. "Who are they?"

"The members of the board of directors," Stubbs said. "The new, merged board. Some were members of the board of the old Guardian Corporation. Some have come over from the network. The new ones were the ones who let Colley sell them a bill of goods. But several of them aren't happy about it."

"What is this bill of goods, Mr. Stubbs?"

"That he, with a free hand, could put *The Guardian* back on top again. Not the same *Guardian*, of course. Spruced up. A magazine with more gimmicks than *Craddock's*. Which, if it could be done at all, would cost one hell of a lot of money. Tax loss for UBN, sure. But—that much of a tax loss? And, come to that, some of the old-line board members, the ones from the original Guardian Corporation, want the magazine to go along pretty much the way it is. After all, it is in the black. Not by a lot, but in the black. And maybe some of them just like the old girl, even if her skirt does come down below her knees."

"But the board did vote for Colley's plan?"

"Not by much of a margin. Sort of an 'oh, all right, give the man his chance. He's been a good man before. Cleared out dead wood before and got away with it.'"

"In effect," Bernie Simmons said, "a personal vote of confidence?"

"Comes to that," Stubbs said. "By a narrow margin. Not everybody thinks Colley's a genius. As he thinks he is." He paused. He said, "Wrong tense, isn't it, gentlemen?"

"As of some time between seven and eight this evening, yes," Simmons told him. "How do you know about this setup, Mr. Stubbs? Is it common gossip?"

"No. Not so far as I know, anyway. How I know is a couple of men on the board are friends of mine."

"What will happen now, do you think? With Colley dead?"

"Perhaps," Stubbs said, "they'll try to pull another genius out of a hat. But I doubt it, Mr. Simmons."

"A one-man operation? In a corporation as big as UBN?"

"For UBN," Stubbs said, "*The Guardian* is small potatoes. And the one-man operation isn't unheard of anywhere. Did you think it was?"

"No," Simmons said. "I've heard tell, Mr. Stubbs. The D.A.'s office comes across it now and then. Did you pass this word along, Mr. Stubbs? The information your friends on the board gave you? That Colley had to prove he was a genius or else, if that's what it came to?"

"No, I didn't. I was told in confidence."

"Not to people on the editorial staff? Not even to Mr. Meade?"

Stubbs smiled. It was a thin smile. Then he said, "Oil and water." Stein and Bernie Simmons looked at each other and both lifted shoulders. It was Stein who said, "Have to ask you to come again, Mr. Stubbs."

"Business and the editorial staffs," Stubbs said. "The way it's always been since I've been here. Probably since Meade's been here, which is one hell of a long time. The way Meade insisted it be. Never the twain shall meet."

Stubbs had, Bernie thought, a rather unusual affinity for tag ends.

"What it came to," Stubbs said, "anybody from the business side had to have a pass to come up here. Up to the genius section. Particularly people in the advertising department. No contamination by crass commercialism. If the advertisers didn't like what *The Guardian* printed they could lump it."

"Did they?"

"Once or twice. Piece a while back about bread. No bread like the old homemade kind. Supposed to be funny. One account—has a baking subsidiary among other things—didn't think it was so damn funny. Another—same comic wrote it—about modern packaging. Advertisers who sell products in packages weren't exactly convulsed. I did get through to Meade on that and he damn near took my ears off. Put it this way, Meade isn't interested in the business side."

"So you didn't bother him with what you'd been told about Colley? And none of the others on this floor? On the editorial staff?"

"I told you," Stubbs said. "I got the word in confidence."

"Mr. Stubbs, did you see this coming? As it affected you, I mean," Stein asked the smallish, resolute man. "Because of what you'd been told about Colley's rather precarious status?"

"Put it this way," Stubbs said, "it wasn't a flabbergasting surprise. Couple of days ago I asked my lawyer if he was sure there aren't any loopholes in my contract. He was."

"So whatever happens, you're all right? If UBN does pull another Colley-type genius out of a hat, or if it doesn't?"

"More than a year to run," Stubbs said. "They buy it up, I'll have plenty of time to look around. Probably won't have to look very far. Sure I'm all right, Mr. Simmons."

Simmons and John Stein consulted briefly, without words. It was Stein who thanked H. R. Stubbs for coming in and said, again, that they were sorry they had had to put him to the trouble. Stubbs said, "Anything I can do," and was told that they would remember that. And they watched the erect man walk out of the office.

"Puts rather a different light on things," Stein said, when the door had closed behind Stubbs. "If what Stubbs says is true. If Colley had persuaded the corporation to let him run a one-man show. If somebody thought that with Colley out of the way things would go along here as they've been going. Things and jobs."

"Yes," Bernie said, "brings in *cui bono*, doesn't it? Something we've been lacking, Johnny. Quite a few who may benefit. If, of course, they knew what Stubbs says he knew. Not just somebody blowing up and bashing on the spur of a nasty moment."

"The six he fired," Stein said. "If we leave Stubbs himself in and include the professor. Who did, apparently, make a grab for that damned statue. Why the hell put a steel rod on that, do you suppose? Something made of plaster would have done just as well."

"Only the best materials for a master angler," Simmons said. "Plaster might break off. Speaking of why the hells, Johnny—why the hell the recorder? Just so Colley could play back his imperishable words—'You're fired'? Doesn't seem to hold water."

"Apparently," Stein said, "he was a strange guy, Colley. Bit of megalomania."

"Need it to be a genius," Simmons said. "I suppose it could be that simple."

He did not sound convinced.

"Anyway," Stein said, "it comes in handy for us."

"Yes," Bernie said. "Very handy. Thing is, Johnny, was that somebody's idea? To make things nice and handy for the police? And—to box us in?"

"Let's not be cryptic, Bernie. Let's not sound like Stubbs, who, incidentally, is a bit of a Colley himself, wouldn't you say?"

"Junior grade," Simmons said. "To give us a tight little group of suspects, six in number. On the theory that they will satisfy us."

"Meaning, obviously, that the killer—whoever was getting ready to be the killer—could have been the one who turned the recorder on. Wouldn't Colley have noticed it?"

"None of the others did, apparently. Obviously the professor didn't. Wouldn't have tried to lie to us if he'd known we had the tape, Johnny. Miss Curran didn't. If Stubbs did he didn't mention it. And—it isn't too difficult to slip out of a party, Johnny. Making sure, in this case, that a man named Colley is still at it, not in his office. It's no trick to turn a recorder on."

"Risk of running into this secretary he'd brought along? This Miss—" He had to consult a typewritten sheet— "Miss Adele Pickett? Who might have been there doing secretarial chores."

"Not if she was in sight at the party. At the same time Colley was. On the other hand—"

Bernie Simmons looked for some seconds over Stein's head.

"Do we know where Miss Pickett lives?" Simmons asked, after his study of the wall behind Lieutenant Stein.

"We know where they all live. And that Robert Fremont, who's one of those on the platter, wasn't home twenty minutes ago, and that his sister is worried about him. And that Kent Simpson, who used to be fiction editor until this afternoon, isn't at home in New Canaan. He and his wife are out. The maid doesn't know where, or says she doesn't. Anything else you think maybe we've slipped up on, Counselor?"

Bernie Simmons let that ride. He said, "And this Miss Pickett, Johnny?"

Stein got up from the desk and went to the door to the

adjacent office. He opened it and said, "Miss Pickett's line still busy, Paul?"

"Seems to be having a nice long chat with somebody," Paul Lane said from the next room. "Or, could be, of course, she's taken it off the hook. Fremont's showed up at his apartment. Only, according to his sister, he's unwell. She thinks he may have eaten something that disagreed with him."

Stein went back and sat behind Jefferson Meade's desk and said, "So, Bernie. We twiddle our thumbs for a while?"

"You know," Bernie Simmons said, "I think we're getting sedentary, Lieutenant. Where does our Miss Pickett live?"

Stein looked it up. He said, "West Fifty-seventh."

"Let's go over and interrupt this chat of hers," Simmons said. "Have a little chat of our own. O.K., Johnny?"

It was O.K. with Lieutenant John Stein.

It was also O.K. with Stein for Bernie Simmons to make a telephone call before they went to chat with Adele Pickett. Sure, Stein told Simmons, it would be a good idea to give Miss Curran a ring. He didn't doubt she was an observant young woman; a young woman who would have noticed if Colley and Miss Pickett were, once or several times, simultaneously at the party, thus leaving a coast clear. He turned Meade's desk and the telephone on it over to the deputy chief of the D.A.'s Homicide Bureau. His smile was friendly and somewhat tolerant.

"Wipe it off, Johnny," Bernie said and sat behind the desk and spun the dial. Spun the dial and waited, and as he waited the responsive smile he had turned on for John Stein became a fixed smile and then faded out. Finally, he cradled the telephone. Stein didn't need to say anything but he said, "No soap, Bernie?"

He saw a line of concentration, and of worry, etch itself between Bernie Simmons's red eyebrows; noticed the slowness with which Simmons shook his head.

"She's had a bad time," Stein said. "What with this business about her sister and then getting fired. Probably she's taken a sleeping pill, Bernie."

"Not like her," Bernie said. "But, could be, I suppose."

"She hadn't planned to go out anywhere?"

She hadn't said anything about such a plan, Bernie told him. Then he said, "Suppose we—"

"Sure," Stein said. "We'll drop by just to check. Give Miss Pickett time to finish her telephone call."

They went in a squad car, with a uniformed driver. The formality of a uniform can be useful and persuasive.

When the car stopped in front of the apartment house, Bernie said he wouldn't be a minute and was told to take his time.

Fred, the doorman—in shirt sleeves but with his uniform cap handy in case of emergency—was tilted back in a chair just inside the entrance doors. He clicked the chair down to the floor and reached for his cap and then said, "Oh, evening, Mr. Simmons."

Bernie agreed it was evening. He said, "Give Miss Curran a buzz, will you, Fred?"

"No use," Fred said. "She went out maybe an hour ago. Car called for her—big Caddy. Chauffeur and everything. I gave her a buzz and she came right down and got in the car. Knew it was coming for her, way it looked."

"Whose car, Fred?"

Fred shrugged his shoulders. Nobody had told him whose car it was. The chauffeur had just asked him to tell Miss Curran that the car was waiting. "So I did."

"She could have come back," Bernie said. "Maybe you went to the head or something."

"Been right here since she left," Fred said. "Been awake, too. She hasn't come back."

"All the same," Bernie Simmons said, "give her a buzz, Fred."

Fred went to the house phone panel and pressed a button and kept his finger on it. He did this several times. He said, "I told you, Mr. Simmons. Nope."

"Suppose we got up and you let me in," Simmons said. "I'd like to have a look."

"Not supposed to," Fred said. "But I guess, being it's you, it'll be all right. Only she ain't there, Mr. Simmons."

It did not take long in the small, moderately cool, apartment on the fifth floor to prove that Nora Curran wasn't there, and to prove that everything in the apartment was as orderly as it had been earlier in the evening. Nora had rinsed out the glasses they had used then; the glasses were upside down on a drainboard. Nora had emptied the ashtrays and rinsed them, too. There wasn't any note wound into the typewriter in the bedroom. There wasn't anything, including—most especially including—a slight young woman with dark brown hair and eyes.

When Bernie got back into the police sedan Stein did not say "No soap, Bernie?" He could tell from looking at the deeper line between red eyebrows that there wasn't any soap.

"Car came for her," Bernie said. "Big Cadillac with chauffeur. Any of our clients run to that?"

"Now that, Bernie, we haven't got to," Stein said. "Probably a lot of chauffeur-driven Cadillacs attached to UBN. And there are also Carey cars, Bernie. We could give them a buzz, I guess."

Simmons shook his head. He didn't own the girl. Until that evening the idea of "owning" that girl hadn't entered his mind. He didn't say this. He said, "Let's drop in on la Pickett," and they drove cross town to West Fifty-seventh Street.

This apartment house was tall and solid and appeared relatively new. The man who opened the door of the police car for them was fully uniformed. He looked with obvious interest at the uniformed policeman behind the wheel. He didn't say anything about that.

The lobby was carpeted and air-conditioned. There was a desk and the clerk behind it wore a neat gray suit. And who should he say was calling on Miss Pickett? Stein told him who to say. The clerk used a telephone. He turned from it and said, "Miss Pickett says about what, Lieutenant?"

"Tell her," Bernie Simmons said, "about Mr. Colley. About the late Mr. Colley, tell her."

The clerk told her. "She says, all right if you have to," he told the tall dark man and the man with such noticeably red hair. He said, "Sixteen D. Either of the elevators on the left."

The elevator operator was also in uniform. A fan whirred in the elevator. The sixteenth-floor corridor was carpeted in green. 16D was at the end of it.

The slender, rather tall woman who opened the door to the limit of the safety chain wore a tailored house-coat and stood noticeably erect. She had black hair and almost black eyes and she was younger than Simmons had expected, although he had no special reason to expect anything about her age. She had, Bernie Simmons thought, been crying.

There were no tears left in her clear voice. She said, "I suppose you have some identification?"

Stein showed her his badge and his ID card. She released the safety chain and they went into a big room, one side of which was glass. Through the glass much of the Borough of Manhattan was hazily bright. There was a fireplace in one wall of the big room and a low, modern sofa faced it, with low, but not matching chairs to make a comfortable fireplace box. All very decorator style, Bernie thought. Also expensive style. UBN must pay the secretary of its trouble-shooter very well indeed. Not trouble-shooter, really. Money man. That probably was what, essentially, Bryan Colley had been.

There was a piano opposite the fireplace group and what Bernie took to be a picture of some sort lying face down on it. A photograph, at a guess; a photograph in a silver frame.

"Sorry to bother you, Miss Pickett," Stein said. "You'd heard about Mr. Colley?"

"It was on the radio," she said, her voice still cool and clear and steady. "It's—it's shocking, Lieutenant. Utterly shocking. He was a wonderful man. Who could have—"

She stopped speaking and her lips, which had been beautifully applied, trembled a little for an instant. She moistened them with the tip of her tongue.

"We're trying to find out," Stein said. "It looks as if it might be one of those he discharged this afternoon. You know about that, of course."

"Yes," she said. "I am—was—his personal secretary, Lieutenant. I knew everything he did. Had to do. I mean of course, everything in connection with his work."

"Of course," Stein said. "This afternoon his work seems to have been firing people."

"Somebody had to," she said. "It was—it was impersonal, Lieutenant. The clearing out of dead wood. It's one of those unpleasant duties which fall to men in Mr. Colley's position."

"Dead wood, Miss Pickett?" Simmons said.

The three of them still were standing only a little way inside the door of the big room.

"I'm afraid so," she said. "Poor Mr. Meade had—allowed it to accumulate. Not, I'm sure, that they aren't all quite capable in their way. But—shouldn't we sit down, gentlemen?"

She walked toward the fireplace grouping and sat on the sofa facing the fireplace. Stein followed her and sat in the nearer of the two chairs. Bernie Simmons went down the room behind the sofa and behind Adele Pickett. His hand was quick as he lifted the silver frame which lay flat on the piano. A photograph was framed in it—the photograph of a man. And, across it, in firm and decisive script, the man had written, "With all my love, Bryan."

She had had time to hide it, Bernie thought, putting the framed photograph down where it had been and being careful that it did not click against the polished wood. Probably forgot it until we rang the doorbell. Did the next best thing. Not a very good thing.

He walked on and around the sofa to the chair which faced the one in which Stein was sitting, leaning a little forward toward the black-haired, polished woman in a somewhat severely tailored house-coat. Severity only house-coat-deep? Bernie wondered, and thought it might be. He picked up Stein's question.

"Capable," Stein said. "But the new management—which seems, from what we hear, to have been largely Mr. Colley himself—didn't think they would fit into the new plans for the magazine?"

"*The Guardian* had been going down hill for several years," Adele Pickett said. "Everybody knows that, Lieutenant. Magazines have to keep up with the times. *The Guardian* has been stagnating, getting even more stuffy. And, slipping backward. Circulation down. Advertising revenue down."

Stein said they had gathered that and also that Bryan Colley had been elected the man to change it.

"He would have," Adele Pickett said. "He'd have put it on top again."

"Only," Simmons said, "we understand he wasn't a magazine man, Miss Pickett. Not primarily."

"A man as capable as Bryan was can take over anything. The details don't matter to men like Br—Mr. Colley. Not that there are many of them."

Had she any idea who, now, would preside over the resurrection of *The Guardian*? She had not. But putting *The Guardian* back on its feet would still be the goal for UBN? She supposed so. She lifted her shoulders and spread her hands. The movement lifted pointed breasts under the house-coat. He had, Bernie thought, been right about the surface depth of severity.

"You are employed by the network," Stein said. "I mean, not by Mr. Colley personally?"

"Of course."

Stein looked around the big room as if he were seeing it for the first time. He looked back at the trim, black-haired woman on the sofa. She sat with knees touching and feet in high-heeled gold mules neatly together. She was not, he noticed, wearing stockings. It occurred to him, as it had some time before occurred to Bernie Simmons, that Adele Pickett might not be wearing anything at all under the tailored house-coat. But her face was artfully put on and, at a guess, recently put on. And, not hurriedly, to meet policemen.

"Yes, Lieutenant," Adele Pickett said, "they do pay me quite well. Mine is an executive position." She smiled at him. She said, "Since you were about to ask."

Stein smiled back, slightly. He said, "Was I, Miss Pickett?" Then he said, "What Mr. Simmons and I came to ask you about is another matter. Did Mr. Colley have you turn on the tape recorder?"

She said, "Tape recorder?" as if the words were new to her.

"On his desk," Stein said, patience in his voice. "Because, you see, it was running all the time he was interviewing the members of the staff he had decided were dead wood."

She shook her head. She said, "Why would he do that?"

"We're trying to find out," Stein said. "Convenient for us, as it turns out. Because it makes it possible for us to check up on the people he fired. Compare their accounts of what happened with what the tape proves did happen."

"You think it was one of those he had to let go?"

"Quite possibly," Stein said. "It's rather pointed out to us, isn't it, Miss Pickett. So you didn't know the recorder was running?"

"No."

"Didn't hear it when you were taking people into the office Mr. Colley was using?"

"It makes almost no sound when it's running. None, really."

"I suppose," Stein said, "that there were times this afternoon when the office Mr. Colley was using was empty? I mean, when neither you nor he was in it?"

"Early," she said, "we were both at the party, off and on."

"The office door wasn't locked?"

"No. Why should it be?" But then her almost black eyes narrowed and she said, "Oh. Why would anybody?"

"Conceivably," Bernie Simmons said, "to help the police. And the District Attorney's office, of course. Conceivably, to help them in the wrong direction."

She nodded her coiffed head slowly. She added that she could see what he meant.

"Miss Pickett," Simmons said, "do you know another man whose first name is Bryan? Not too common a first name. Spelled with a 'Y' at any rate. A man, say, who would inscribe a photograph to you? 'With all my love'?"

He did not wait for an answer. He got up and went to the piano and brought back with him the silver-framed photograph. He took it to John Stein, who looked at it and said, "Yes, Bernie." Then he said, "Well, Miss Pickett?"

She put her elbows on her knees and her face in her raised

hands. And for a moment her slim body shook. But then she sat straight again. She said, "Can't you leave me alone? Can't you? What does it matter?"

"No," Simmons said. "We can't leave anybody alone, Miss Pickett. I don't know, neither of us knows, whether it matters. Well?"

"Bryan and I were married," she said. "For more than two years. And—and he was coming back to me tonight. Tonight. Tonight!"

Again she put her face in her lifted hands, and again her body shook. She did not, this time, quickly sit erect again. When she did, finally, she still made small sobbing sounds and her eyes were wet.

VIII

What they had, they agreed half an hour later, was the obvious, was a triangle. Triangles are frequent in murder cases. On this, sitting in the police car, they also agreed. The next person to have a chat with was Miss Rosalie Shaffner. On that they agreed. But it was evident by then that Miss Shaffner herself did not share in the agreement. A telephone call from the car to Paul Lane, then back at Homicide North, settled that.

Miss Shaffner had not gone home to her apartment. She had gone to the Grand Central Terminal and taken a late New Haven train—a train which stopped at Greenwich and at Stamford and continued on to New Haven. The detective who was keeping an eye on her had had time to call in before he joined her on the train.

Adele Pickett, in the half hour after she had told them she was Adele Colley, had told them several other things.

Yes, she knew there had been, for about a year, another woman Bryan Colley had been seeing. "Some woman he left me for." She denied she knew who the other woman was, and Simmons and Stein did not tell her who it almost certainly was. Bryan had got tired of this other woman and had said he was coming home to Adele. That evening he had been coming and she had gone to the apartment and waited—waited and turned on the radio and heard that he was not coming, that night or any night.

She had not been talking on the telephone. There must be something wrong with the telephone if it had sounded the busy signal. "After I—after I heard I just sat. I don't know what I did. Perhaps I made myself a drink."

There was a telephone extension in the living room. Its receiver was secure in the cradle. Another telephone? There was one in the bedroom and Stein went to check it. There the receiver was not secure. It was only half in the cradle, propped against one of the blunt prongs. The dial tone sounded from it.

"She could," Simmons said in the car, "have wanted us to call in person. To show how she had dressed—undressed—for a returning husband. Proving she expected him to return. Proving she hadn't hit him over the head when, perhaps, he told her he had changed his mind about being a prodigal."

Stein agreed to that. And they agreed that Rosalie Shaffner, simultaneously discharged from love and from occupation, was equally likely to be upset, conceivably to the point of violence. They would ask her about that when she returned from her trip, wherever her trip took her. When she returned or was brought back.

"A couple of days ago she and Bryan Colley broke up," Stein said, making it clear on the record. "If Adele is telling the truth, Colley was the one who broke it off. He may have told her he was going back to his wife. Being fired after that could have been the last straw."

It was Rosalie Shaffner who, ignoring suggestions, had left town. It was Adele Colley, nee Pickett, who had put on a show for them. Or might have put on a show for them. Might have gone to her expensive apartment after murdering, put a telephone receiver askew in its cradle and dressed, undressed, to receive company, which would almost certainly come if it could not telephone.

"Pay your money and take your choice," Stein said. "I wonder if Miss Curran is home yet?"

Bernie Simmons had also been wondering. He looked at his watch. A quarter after eleven. Late, but murder does not keep regular hours. They drove across town.

The apartment house door was locked and a dim light showed in the lobby. Simmons found the night bell and pressed on it and they waited. They had to wait several minutes before Fred, wearing trousers, a skivvy shirt, slippers and an expression of disapproval, came to open the door for them.

"People who forget their—" he began and then said, "Oh, hello, Mr. Simmons. She came back."

It was several minutes before there was an answer to the buzzing of the house phone in Apartment 5J. When the answer came it was not in a sleepy voice; when Bernie spoke into the transmitting grill, Nora's voice was quick. "I tried to get you," she said. "At *The Guardian* they said you and the lieutenant had gone. Of course, come up."

"Sounded a little excited," Stein said, as they went up in the elevator. He was told that everybody using that announcing system sounded excited—raspingly excited.

Nora opened the door quickly, as if she had been standing with her hand on the knob.

"Bernie," Nora said, "I've got my job back."

In the coolish living room, she told them how she had got her job back, got a better job in exchange for the old one. She told them all of it—all except the nagging uneasiness she had felt when Meade first telephoned her. That wasn't important any longer; it had been absurd from the start.

"Very clear," Simmons said when she had finished. "You're a very clear girl, Nora. Agreed, Johnny?"

"Very clear," Stein said. "The whole thing must have come as a surprise to you, Miss Curran."

"A tremendous surprise."

"You hadn't known that Mr. Simpson was dissatisfied with his job? Wanted to get back to writing?"

"No," Nora said. "Oh, sometimes he said he wondered what he was doing as an editor instead of being a writer. Said he should have stuck to his trade. That sort of thing. But doesn't everybody sometimes wonder about things like that?"

"Second-guess themselves," Bernie said. "Yes. Most people do. But you didn't think—suspect—it was more definite than that with Simpson?"

"No, Bernie. Not really."

"Found a decision made for him," Bernie said. "Suddenly realized it was the right decision. Or, of course, his wife did. Was that what you gathered from what Mr. Meade said?"

"Yes. And, without using those words, I think Mr. Meade felt that too."

"Miss Curran," Stein said, "I know you can't be sure. But do you think Mr. Meade was surprised at the way things have turned out? I mean, that the network is going to abandon, at least for the time being, its plan to change the magazine? Revitalize it, they'd probably say."

"I'm sure he was surprised," she said. "He said he was and—oh, I don't know. Acted as if he was."

"It must have been a very pleasant surprise to him," Stein said. "When I talked to him earlier I got the impression that *The Guardian* is very important to him. Makes up—oh, makes up most of his life. Sort of like getting his life back, this change of mind on the network's part must have seemed. Did you feel anything like that in his attitude?"

"It may have been there, Lieutenant," Nora said. "He didn't—oh, didn't break into song about it. He's not that kind of man. And, I was more or less breaking into song myself. Inside, of course. Thinking more what it meant to me than what it must mean to him."

"Understandably," Stein said. "Mind going over again what Meade said about the chance somebody—the killer—had been waiting in his office? Waiting for the coast to be clear?"

She did not mind. She went over it again.

"But you yourself didn't hear any sounds from Meade's office? While you were in Colley's?"

"No. Of course, I was thinking about what was happening to me. All I was listening to was what was happening to me."

Understandably, Stein said again. "We tried to get in touch with you earlier, Miss Curran. While you were at Meade's house, apparently. You see, this tape recorder thing is puzzling. It occurred to me—occurred to Mr. Simmons too—that somebody might have gone into the office, the office Colley was using, when it was empty. And turned the tape recorder on."

"Why?"

It was, Bernie told her, only guessing on their part. Conceivably to misdirect.

"To," Bernie said, "provide us with a platter of red herrings."

She looked at Bernie and her face changed. There had been animation in her face. That faded out of it.

"You wanted," she said, and now spoke very slowly, "to ask me if I'd sneaked into the office? Turned the recorder on? Oh, I know how. There's one on my desk, too. Turned the one on in Colley's office to misdirect you and the lieutenant here? The answer is, I didn't, Mr. Simmons."

Bernie was shaking his head long before she finished; shaking his head at her and smiling at her. When she stopped and looked at him—in effect glared at him—he said, "Take it easy, child." (He got for that, as he expected, "Don't call me *child!*")

"Only," Stein said, "whether you had seen both Mr. Colley and Miss Pickett at the party at the same time, Miss Curran. Which would have left the office open for anyone to go in."

She said, "Oh," and for some seconds did not add to that.

"I think so," she said. "But it's nothing I could swear to, Lieutenant. Early on in the party I think I saw both of them at it. Not together. Mr. Colley was with a group of men I'd never seen before—men from the network, I thought. I think I saw Miss Pickett talking to someone. I don't remember who."

The smile came back to her face suddenly, and with it some of the animation which had been there.

"I didn't," Nora said, "know I was being a witness."

"People don't, more's the pity," Bernie said. "Well, Johnny? Think we ought to let the lady get some sleep?"

John Stein stood up. There was no special expression in his dark face or in his dark eyes. He said, "Thank you, Miss Curran. You've been helpful," and turned and walked across the room toward the door. She said, "Good night, Lieutenant," after him and then, in a different tone, "Good night, Bernie. I'm sorry I—"

He put an arm around her shoulders. He smiled down at her. He said, "Good night, child," and followed Stein.

"So now?" Bernie said, in the car, to John Stein. It was almost dark in the car with the doors closed. A little light came in from the street.

"Bernie," Stein said, "You're sure you want to go on being in on this? If you like, we can hold things up for a while. Until morning, say. Give you a chance to pick somebody else from your bureau. Or just let us handle it until we ask your office to approve a charge."

"Now, why the hell?" Bernie said.

"Because," Stein said, "you've fallen for the pretty girl, haven't you, Bernie? Which could blur things a little for you, couldn't it? And—make things awkward for you."

"Trouble with you, Johnny, you're nuts," Bernie Simmons said. "There's nothing to make things awkward for me."

"*Cui bono*," Stein said. "Also, it's an ill wind. Also, Counselor, the matter of a locked door. I told you that, early on. The door between the two offices. Which leaves only one door to open, doesn't it? The door to a corridor. A corridor Miss Curran didn't see anybody in. Anybody waiting until she came out of Colley's office to go in when she came out."

"Why come out, Lieutenant? And then go back?"

"Oh," Stein said, "to see that there wasn't anybody in the corridor, Counselor. Sometimes people yell when they're getting killed. Natural thing to do. Awkward for a killer if there are people near enough to come running if they hear a yell. Add it up, Counselor."

"All right," Bernie Simmons said, "I see your figures, Johnny. And I can add. But—we don't come to the same total. So—let's go pay a call on Mr. Meade. Apparently he doesn't mind late hours."

They drove across town and a few blocks uptown and parked, behind a dark Cadillac, in front of a narrow, private house. They went up three scrubbed white steps, with a brass rail on either side, and rang a doorbell.

The man in the white jacket who opened for them the

front door of a narrow house did not seem surprised, nor did he behave as if the hour were late. He said he was quite sure that Mr. Meade had not retired and that, if the lieutenant and Mr. Simmons would come in, he'd see if Mr. Meade was—

He did not need to. Meade stood, lean and tall, in the doorway between entrance hall and living room. He smiled at them. He said, "Come in, gentlemen, and ask your questions." They went into a narrow, cool living room. He offered them drinks, but both shook their heads. He pointed to chairs and, when they were seated, sat himself in a chair beside a small table with a half-emptied glass on it.

"We understand, Mr. Meade," Bernie Simmons said, "that you had a surprise this evening. A pleasant surprise."

"News gets around, doesn't it?" Meade said. "Simpson? Or—Miss Curran, Counselor?"

"Miss Curran told us you sent a car for her," Stein said. "I gather you telephoned the others?"

"Kent Simpson," Meade said. "Tried poor Fremont. His sister says he's indisposed. Her way of putting it, I'm afraid. I got Cliff Armstrong and told him he had his office back, for now, anyway. Miss Shaffner doesn't answer her phone."

"You telephoned the others," Bernie Simmons said. "Sent a car to pick Miss Curran up. Why the difference, Mr. Meade?"

"Miss Curran's case was—is—rather special. She probably told you that. Instead of being discharged, she's being promoted. I wanted to see how she took it. And that she would take it. The new job, I mean. Whether she thought she was up to it. As I do. Also, she lives only a few blocks away."

"Mr. Meade," Bernie said, "you had no inkling that Mr. Colley's death would make this difference? That it was so much a one-man operation that UBN would abandon it with him dead?"

"None," Meade said. "I assumed that they would, of course, send somebody else. Also, Mr. Simmons, I suspect that 'abandon' is too strong a word. Much too final a word. 'Postpone' is the word I'd use. It is, I'm afraid, a reprieve for *The Guardian*. And for all of us. Not a pardon."

"You've no idea whether anybody else—anybody on the staff—knew, or guessed, that with Colley dead the magazine would go on as it had been going? At least temporarily?"

Stein asked that. And to that Meade gravely shook his head.

"It seems to me unlikely that any of them did," Meade said. "Most unlikely."

"Not Stubbs?"

"Not so far as I know," Meade said, and lifted his glass and sipped from it and looked over it, not at either of the two he sat with. Then he said, "Of course, Stubbs is in a different category. A business man. More in contact, I suppose, with the business men who are members of our board. He may have been in a better position to guess what would happen."

"But he didn't guess in your presence, Mr. Meade?" Bernie asked him.

Again Meade shook his head.

"Actually," he said, "I seldom saw him. At *The Guardian* there's a line drawn. Business office on one side, editorial staff on the other. The way I think it should be."

"Have you any idea why Colley would want a recording of his interviews this afternoon?"

"None," Meade said. "It seems an odd thing to want. I can't imagine why he did it. Lieutenant, during the interviews you speak of did any of the people get—let's say excited? Threatening?"

"One or two took it rather hard," Stein said. He did not amplify, although Meade looked expectant. "I suppose you didn't overhear anything from the next office? While Colley was telling people they were through at *The Guardian*?"

"Nothing. The door between the offices is heavy, lieutenant. Also, I wasn't in my office except briefly. At the party most of the time. Felt I should be. When I felt I'd done all that was required, I went back to my office for a minute or two. Put a few papers in the desk drawer."

"Was Colley in his office then?" Simmons asked.

"I don't know. The door was closed. The corridor door, I mean."

Could he be more precise than he had been about what time it was when he was in his office? Before he decided to go home and change for his dinner?

He thought about six-thirty. Thought it was about then when he locked up and left.

"Locked up?" Bernie said. "You locked your office when you left?"

"Always do," Meade said. "Both doors. The cleaning women have master keys. And are very responsible people."

"Both doors?" Bernie said. "The one to the corridor? And the one between your office and the one Colley was using?"

"Of course I—" Meade said and stopped abruptly and snapped his fingers. Then he said, "Forgot that."

"When you were talking to Miss Curran?" Stein said. "According to what she told us you thought somebody—presumably whoever killed Colley—might have been hiding in your office. Waiting, you thought—she says you said were 'afraid'—until the time was right. To use the connecting door and go into Colley's office. Only—"

"Oh," Meade said, "I'm ahead of you, Lieutenant. I'd forgotten I'd locked the door when I said that. A reflex to lock the doors. Nothing that made any impression on my mind."

"So to get from your office to Colley's somebody would have had to have a key? Did you leave yours where anybody could get it?"

For answer, Meade took a leather key container out of his pocket and flicked it open and shook one of several keys loose in it. He let it dangle in sight. He amplified the obvious by saying, "Here it is, Lieutenant."

"Did Colley have a key to the door?" Bernie asked the man who was putting the key folder back into his pocket.

"No. Of course, the door wasn't locked ordinarily during working hours. Barclay—he was managing editor until recently —and I used to pop in on each other."

"But it could be locked only from your side?"

"Yes."

"So nobody who might have been waiting his chance in your office really would have had a chance," Bernie Simmons said. "Unless he had a key."

"That's right," Meade said. "That's entirely right. Want me to finish it for you, Counselor? I had a key. I could have gone into the other office and hit Colley over the head. Only, I didn't, Counselor. And I was home—here—changing for a dinner party. And—is it clear when poor Colley was killed, Lieutenant?"

"Some time between seven and eight," Stein said. "Yes, Mr. Meade, we know you got home at about a quarter of seven. And went up to your bedroom to change. And came down, changed, at a few minutes after eight. And got into your car, which Alfred had brought around earlier, and were driven uptown to your party."

"Yes," Meade said and smiled pleasantly at Lieutenant Stein. "Alfred told me your men had checked. And wanted to double-check with Brenda. And couldn't because I'd given her the afternoon off, since I wasn't going to be here for dinner. I hope Alfred didn't have any trouble remembering?"

"None," Stein said. "Seems to have been very clear about everything."

He turned to Bernie Simmons and said, "Think of anything else we want to ask Mr. Meade, Counselor?"

Bernie Simmons said he couldn't think of anything else they needed to ask Mr. Meade. He added, "At the moment."

IX

Back in the police car it was Stein's suggestion that they call it a night. "It," which was the investigation of the violent death of one Bryan Colley, would continue without them. It was in the hopper, and the hopper of the Police Department does not sleep. Men must, Stein pointed out, and suggested he drop Simmons at his apartment and have the car turned in and go home himself. Bernie Smmons said, "I guess so, Johnny," in a tone which suggested he was thinking of something else.

In front of the apartment house it was Simmons who suggested that Stein come up for a drink. "I don't know," Stein said and then, "All right, Bernie. I guess I will." He told the patrolman to check the car in and then went up to Bernie Simmons's three-room apartment and Bernie made them drinks and they stretched out, two long men in two low chairs. For some time neither of them said anything. Then Simmons said, "All right, Johnny. Get it said."

"I have," Stein said. "For my money we've enough for a charge. Enough to take before a grand jury. Want to go over it again?"

"Nora Curran, spinster, age twenty-six, assistant fiction editor of a magazine called *The Guardian*, is in need of money," Simmons said, with no expression whatever in his voice. "She gets fired by an objectionable man and goes off her rocker and kills him. She knows in advance—or guesses in advance—that with him dead she'll get back a job she needs. Perhaps she guesses, too, that a man named Kent Simpson wants to quit editing and go back to writing.

"Succinct," Stein said. "Plus an opening door which could only have been one door. Plus an empty corridor. And, before you say it, Bernie, we know the corridor was empty only because she says it was. But she couldn't say that John Smith, or Robert Fremont or H. R. Stubbs was coming along it, obviously heading for Colley's office, because John Smith might be able to prove he was—oh, at the bar. Or having an interesting conversation with five other people."

"The communicating door was locked when you got there, Johnny? Find another key to open it?"

"Lane has a gimmick," Stein said. "No, we haven't found any other key. Several keys among Colley's effects. None of them fitted. The only one we know about is in Meade's pocket. Unless he's emptied his pockets and taken off his trousers and gone to bed." He drank and lighted a cigarette and said he'd better call in. He called in and after a few minutes came back to his chair and his drink.

There wasn't, he said, anything particularly new. The man who was keeping an eye on Rosalie Shaffner had not reported. H. R. Stubbs had got home safely. The light in Nora Curran's window was out. Robert Fremont's telephone rang unanswered.

"Enough to go on, for my money," John Stein said, and was told that he had said that before. And that whether there was enough to go on was for the District Attorney's office to decide. "And at the moment," Bernie Simmons said, "I'm the D.A.'s office."

"Also, you're Bernard Simmons, a man who's fallen for a girl. Aren't you, Counselor?"

"Incompetent, irrelevant and immaterial," Bernie said. "Speaking as a counselor at law. And, speaking as deputy chief, Homicide Bureau, office of the District Attorney, County of New York, we haven't got enough. Not even for an indictment. Almost certainly, not enough for a conviction, and the chief doesn't like acquittals. Not that he wants to convict the innocent, but—"

"I know," Stein said. "That he doesn't want the innocent to come to trial. Ever occur to you, Bernie—long as we're letting our hair down—that he doesn't like conflict of interest among members of his staff?"

"If it ever got that far," Bernie said, "I could, as a defense lawyer, get her off with both hands tied behind my back. I'd say there was a woman named Adele Pickett, who hadn't spread it around that she was really Adele Colley and who had cause for jealousy. And that there was another woman named Rosalie Shaffner, who also had. And a man named Clifford Armstrong, who is a spluttery type and who was popping in and out of office at the time Colley was killed. And—hell, Johnny, I could go on and on."

"A locked door that couldn't be opened, Bernie. And a door that was. Within seconds of its closing. And a tape to play to a jury."

"Which might very well be held inadmissible," Simmons said. "No, Lieutenant."

"Motive," Stein said. "What amounts to exclusive opportunity. Means—that damned trophy handy on the desk."

"My client," Bernie said, "takes the stand. She denies she had any idea that the death of Bryan Colley would be of advantage to her. Denies she had ever heard rumors that Colley's was a one-man operation. Denies that she had any idea Kent Simpson wouldn't want his job back, or that she would get it if he didn't want it. Denies that she went back into the office after she left it."

"Last person known to have been in the office," Stein said. "Tape recording stops after she leaves. By your own admission, Miss Curran, there was nobody waiting to go in after you left. Mr. Meade to the stand. 'You are quite certain, Mr. Meade, that you locked the door between your office and that Mr. Colley was using?' Answer, 'Yes.' 'And that the door could not be opened without a key?' 'Yes, Counselor.' 'And that there was a keyhole only on your side—I mean, of course, your office side? And that you put the key in your pocket after you'd locked the door and took it home with you? When you left at about six-thirty on the evening in question?' I get a lot of yeses for answers, Bernie. Want to cross-examine, Counselor?"

"Yes, Johnny," Bernie Simmons said. "I know you've been

to law school. Very commendable. And that you've got your degree."

"Take my examinations in the fall," Stein said. "Well, Bernie?"

"You checked out with this man of Meade's," Simmons said. "Alfred something."

"Jenkins. Yes. His employer got home at about ten minutes of seven. Went up to his room to change. Turned on his TV to get the seven o'clock news. Jenkins heard it."

"Jenkins saw him come in?"

"Yes."

"And's sure about the time. Did Meade look at his watch and say, 'Well, well, Alfred, here it is ten minutes of seven already? Bear that in mind, will you, in case anybody asks you'?"

"No. He did say, according to Jenkins, that it might be an idea to pick the car up early and park it in front. Because, on Friday evenings especially, there's a stampede at the garage they keep it in. And yes, Bernie. We did find out what garage and find the man who brought the car down. Jenkins picked it up at seven-thirty. Had to wait almost fifteen minutes for it to be brought down. Had to move three cars to get it out, the car jockey did. And Jenkins parked it in front of the house about ten minutes after he got it. And went into the house. And Mr. Meade's shower was running upstairs. It makes a 'gurgle,' Jenkins says. Meade came down from his bedroom at a few minutes after eight and was in dinner clothes. And had nicked himself shaving, but not enough to bother, beyond a little dabbing."

"Observant man, this Jenkins," Simmons said. "Mr. Meade ought to use an electric razor. See any nick when you first talked to him tonight, Johnny?"

"I," Stein said, "am not all that observant. But I'm not Meade's houseman. Just a cop trying to find a killer. And a man, Bernie, who hasn't fallen for a pretty girl."

"Come off it," Simmons said. "I've met your wife. All right. You're a cop. I'm an assistant district attorney. Cooperating in your investigation, as provided. Telling you, officially, that you haven't enough evidence for a charge, against Nora Curran—against anybody."

"O.K.," Stein said. "Sleep on it, Bernie. We'll both sleep on it."

He stood up. And the telephone rang. Simmons went the length of the living room with long strides and into a corridor beyond it. He moved, John Stein thought, like a man who had been expecting, at any rate hoping for, a call from a girl.

But Simmons came back, almost at once. He did not come back as fast as he had gone. He came back to tell Stein that the call was for him, from Paul Lane.

Stein was gone several minutes. He came back slowly and sat down. Then he said, "Remember a man named Henri Pridieux, Bernie?"

Simmons shook his head at first. Then he nodded. "A waiter," he said. "Witness in the Page killing. A witness who never got to testify. Hit and run."

"Yes," Stein said. "We've apparently lost another one, Bernie. Same way as before.* Only this man is named—was named—Fremont. Interesting coincidence, isn't it?"

Bernie Simmons agreed that it was an interesting conicidence. He added that he didn't like coincidences. He was told that, in that case, he'd better brace himself. Because—

"Fremont was killed about half a block from Meade's house," Stein said. "And Meade saw it happen. He was the one who called headquarters. And called an ambulance. And he and Jenkins carried Fremont into the house, which maybe they shouldn't have done, but people don't think of that. And it was D.O.A. Probably it was dead some time before arrival."

He got up from the chair and Simmons came effortlessly out of his, although he was long and the chair was low.

"Too bad you turned the car in," Bernie said. "Hard to find cabs this time of night."

The time was well after midnight. They had to wait al-

* As recounted in *Squire of Death*.

most five minutes before a vacant taxi came along. Time didn't matter too much. Jefferson Meade had already told policemen from a cruise car what had happened. He would have to tell it again.

The police cruiser was just pulling away from the curb in front of Meade's narrow house. The taxi driver banged on his horn ring and the cruiser stopped. "Thought you might want to talk to them, Lieutenant," the taxi driver said. "Patrolman Whipple, sir. Moonlighting. Remember you since you were a sergeant."

"Coincidences buzz all around," Simmons said, and paid Patrolman Whipple, driving a taxi during his off hours. And, according to regulations, wearing his revolver while he drove.

A sergeant got out of the cruise car and walked back to the taxi and said, "Yeah? Got some trouble, Mac?" He peered in at the driver. He said, "Oh, hiyah, Joe. Want something?"

Joe Whipple said, "Nope. Not me. Thought maybe Lieutenant Stein might."

The sergeant had already reported in, and reported that it looked like being just one of those things—hit and run, vehicular homicide by person or persons unknown. Driving a dark car, probably green. Probably a Chevrolet. Witness, owner of that house there—gesture—named Jefferson Meade. Victim—

"We know," Stein told him. "When?"

"Mr. Meade says about midnight," the sergeant said. "Maybe a little before. Meade was, he says—"

"All right," Stein said, "we'll ask him, Sergeant. Could be this ties in with something we're working on."

"Want us to stand by, Lieutenant?" the sergeant asked, and was told they needn't.

Alfred Jenkins opened the door for them, as he had earlier. He was not, now, wearing a white jacket. He was in shirtsleeves, and one of the sleeves of his shirt had blood on it— what looked like blood. He'd see if Mr. Meade—

But Meade was already coming down the stairs which ended in the entrance hall. He wore a dark blue robe. He said,

"Wondered if you two wouldn't show up. It's a bad thing—a terrible thing. If he'd only waited until I routed Alfred out. But—"

"He was here?" Stein said. "Fremont was here?"

"Here," Meade said. "Drunk. Incoherent. We may as well go in and sit down."

He led them into the narrow living room and they sat, much as they had sat before. And, as before, Meade offered them drinks and they refused drinks. He said, "If you don't mind, I need one," and walked the length of the room to a bar and poured from a bottle onto ice. He came back with his drink. He said, "It was so damned needless. If he'd only waited. Alfred would have driven him home."

He was asked to start at the beginning and said, "Of course. Of course. It was only a few minutes after you gentlemen left. I'd told Alfred that that was all for the night and he'd gone to his part of the house. I was just about to go up myself when—"

When, he told them, the doorbell rang. He went to the door and looked out through its glass. "Quiet neighborhood here. All the same." He had seen Fremont through the glass—a small, somewhat weaving figure through the glass. He opened the door, he told them.

Fremont had come in. "Fell in's more like it. He was just able to navigate."

Meade had helped Fremont navigate into the living room. "Half carried him. He didn't weigh much." He put the frail and drunken religious editor into a chair and, at first, thought Fremont was going, instantly, to fall asleep in it. But then Fremont roused himself and began to talk. What he was talking about was his job. What he was talking about was wanting his job back. *Having* to have his job back.

"He babbled," Meade said. "His words were—oh, all mixed up. You both probably know how drunks are."

They knew how drunks could be.

"Begged for his job back," Meade said. "I had a feeling—oh, that he'd have gone down on his knees if he could have made it. He'd lean forward and almost fall out of the chair. Couple of times I had to catch him and push him back. It was all rather dreadful. Degrading. And embarrassing, of course. He just went on and on and wouldn't listen. I kept telling him he still had his job, but he didn't seem to take it in."

Finally, Meade said, he had gone back to the kitchen and made coffee and got Robert Fremont to drink some of it. It had helped a little; at least, he swayed less, sitting in his chair. But he kept on talking; kept on saying the same things over and over. He kept on not listening to assurance that he still had his job.

"Would he have had it?" Bernie Simmons asked. "Because he sounds like one hell of a religious editor."

"I'd never seen him the way he was tonight," Meade said. "I never knew him well. It was Barclay took him on, actually. The managing editor who left us a few weeks ago. I knew Fremont—well, drank a bit. And that he'd lost a couple of charges because of it. But with us he did his work."

"Charges?" Stein said.

"He was an ordained clergyman," Meade said. "Episcopalian. The Reverend Robert Fremont, actually. Signed his pieces that way. Was a vicar in a small church somewhere upstate and was ousted, or whatever they do to clergymen who drink too much. Got another charge and lost it, too. At least, that's what I gathered. Worked on some religious publication for a while. Where Barclay found him, when we needed a religious editor. You asked, Mr. Simmons, whether we would, actually, have kept him on the staff. I'm not at all sure, after tonight's—display."

"He needed the job?"

"Apparently. He made it sound—oh, that he needed it desperately. But, as I say, it was hard to make out what he was trying to say. And impossible to make him understand that he didn't need to say it. That circumstances had changed."

"He never did understand?"

Meade could not be sure. Perhaps, when the coffee had sobered him up a little. "I certainly tried hard enough to get through to him," Meade said. "Was never entirely sure I had.

Then he suddenly stood up. Almost knocked a table over and did spill coffee all over it. He—"

Fremont had walked, still wobbling a good deal, into the entrance hall and begun fumbling with the doorknob, trying to turn it.

"I realized he was in no condition to get home alone," Meade said. "How he'd ever got here I can't imagine. I told him to wait. That I'd get Alfred and have him driven home. He said, 'Make it all right,' or something like that, but he quit fumbling with the knob and I thought I'd finally got through to him, on that, anyway, and went back to get Alfred. His rooms are beyond the kitchen."

Meade had awakened his houseman-chauffeur and told him what was wanted. Then he had gone back into the entrance hall. And found the front door open and Fremont gone.

Meade had gone out the door and stood on the stoop and looked up and down the street.

"He was half a block away," Meade said. "Weaving badly. From one side of the walk to the other. And while I was watching—*while I was watching*—he staggered off the curb. And this car was coming—coming too fast. It was weaving some. Maybe whoever was driving it was as drunk as poor Fremont. Anyway—"

Anyway, the car hit the staggering man. It threw him back on the sidewalk and across it and up against a building.

"He just lay there, crumpled up."

The car had gone on and around the next corner.

"I yelled for Alfred," Meade said. "We both ran up to poor Fremont and carried him back here. There's—there's blood on the floor in the entry hall. But I think he was dead when we picked him up."

Meade had called the police and called for an ambulance. "Everybody was very quick," he said. "But—not quick enough. One of the policemen—a sergeant it was, I think—said we shouldn't have moved him. But we couldn't just leave him lying there. We might have been able to do something for him."

"You did what almost everyone would have done," Stein told him. "This car that killed him. You saw it. Big car? Little car?"

"I was watching poor Fremont," Meade said. "Looking up the street toward him. The car came from behind me and I got, actually, only a glimpse of it—enough to see that it was wavering and going too fast. It was a dark car. I have a feeling it was dark green, but the light wasn't very good. It isn't in this block."

"No idea about the make?"

"Medium-size car. They all look pretty much alike nowadays. To me, anyway."

"You told the sergeant it was probably a Chevrolet. At least he says you did."

"Perhaps I did," Meade said. "Probably I did. I'm afraid I wasn't very clear in my mind just then, Lieutenant."

"Understandably," Stein said. "But it was a dark car, probably green. It could have been a Chevrolet?"

"I think so," Meade said. "Anyway, I thought so then. When I was, in a way, still seeing it—seeing it shooting along the street and hitting Fremont."

"Swerve after it hit him?"

"It seemed to me it just kept on going. Not swerving any more than it had before. But, it all seemed to happen at once, Lieutenant."

"The car had lights on?"

Meade did not remember. But it must have had. Wait—he did remember. The tail lights were on. He didn't remember any fan of lights spreading out in front of the car.

"Could be," Stein said, "he was using just his parking lights. Years ago it used to be legal to drive in town with only those. In which case, of course, the driver—particularly if he'd been drinking—might not have seen Fremont until it was too late. No sound of his putting on brakes, Mr. Meade? Tire sounds, I mean?"

Meade, again, did not remember. He said he was afraid he was a bad witness.

He was as good as most, Stein thought, and did not say.

He did say he supposed Meade had not had any chance to look at the car's rear license plate.

Meade had. It was a New York State plate.

"You can't by any chance, remember the number?"

"Only the start of it. Three N something. I've—oh, only a vague feeling about the rest. It's—say on the tip of my mind."

"The driver? Man or woman?"

"I don't—wait a minute."

Meade looked at the opposite wall and his eyes narrowed a little.

"Again, I'm a bad witness," he said, after a somewhat long pause. "But, I have a feeling—now, trying to remember back, picture back—a feeling that a woman was driving the car. I don't really know why it feels like that. I only, actually, saw the back of a head. But it seems now that it was shaped like a woman's head."

"Long hair? Anything like that?"

Meade shook his own head. He didn't think the driver had had long hair. The driver's head, man's or woman's, was just a shape. In the vague picture in his own mind the shape was that of a woman's head.

"When he was talking about his job," Bernie Simmons said. "Trying to tell you how important it was to him, did you gather it was because he needed the money?"

Meade supposed it was that; almost inevitably it was that. Fremont lived with his sister, Meade thought. Probably supported her, although on that Meade was only guessing.

"He was well paid at *The Guardian*?"

"Quite well, I think. I don't know the exact figure, but the staff is well paid."

"When Colley fired Miss Curran," Simmons said, "he gave her a check for a month's salary. Do you know whether he did that for Fremont?"

Meade said he didn't know, but that he supposed that had been the arrangement.

"You don't sign the checks?"

Meade looked surprised as he shook his head. Checks came out of the business office. They were signed by the treasurer of the corporation. He sighed. "We've got computers now," he said. "I suppose somebody tells a computer."

He took a rather long sip of his drink.

"Actually," he said, "I'm not sure that the loss of his salary was what upset poor Fremont most. A—call it a sense of failure. Of repeated failure. It wasn't clear. Nothing he said was clear. But there was a feeling of a man who had lost more than the money he needed to live on. Of, in a sense, a man who felt he had lost himself. Lost—oh, I don't know how it should be put—had lost the shape of himself."

He smiled slightly and shook his head.

"Not very tangible, is it?" he said. "Not the sort of tangible thing you two want."

"Even in our trade," Simmons said, "there are a good many intangibles, Mr. Meade. Things hard to pin down."

Meade said he supposed so. He finished his drink. He looked suddenly, Bernie thought, very much like a man who would like late visitors to leave so he could go to bed. Bernie looked at John Stein and raised his eyebrows and Stein said, "Yes, Counselor. We've probably bothered Mr. Meade long enough."

"I want to do everything—" Meade said, and stopped that when Stein stood up and then Bernie Simmons stood up.

"I'm sure you want to help in any way you can," Bernie said.

"It was just an accident," Meade said. "Tragic but an accident. I'm sure of that." He stood up too. "Aren't you, gentlemen?"

"It sounds very much like being just that," Stein said. "Just a hit and run. But, a coincidence, wouldn't you say, Mr. Meade?"

"Yes. A tragic one. You—I mean someone in the police department will tell his sister what's happened?"

That probably had already been done, Stein told him, as they walked across the room toward the entry hall. Meade opened the door for them and they started down the three white steps to the sidewalk. After two steps, Simmons turned back.

"By the way," he said, "is that your car, Mr. Meade?" He pointed to a big car parked at the curb.

"Why, yes," Meade said. "I thought Alfred had taken it to the garage long ago. It's not like him to forget."

"Been a disturbing day for everybody," Bernie said. "But, then, murder days always are."

There was no hope for a cab in this by-way. Stein said as much and started off. But Bernie Simmons stopped in front of the Cadillac and bent to look down at, and under, the right front fender. He looked only briefly and stood up again and walked after Lieutenant John Stein.

"Looking for a tangible?" Stein asked him, as they walked toward First Avenue. "Find one?"

"No," Simmons said. "Of course, as Mr. Meade said, this block isn't very well lighted."

X

They walked the quiet cross-town street toward First Avenue. For half a block they walked in silence and then Stein said, "We're agreed on what it looks like, Counselor?"

"It looks," Bernie Simmons said, "like murder, Lieutenant. The murder of a man who might have had something to say. Something somebody didn't want said. Obviously, it needn't be that."

"No," Stein said. "Coincidences are all the time lousing things up. Has Miss Curran a car, Bernie?"

"She leased one in June," Bernie said. "Dr. Werkes has a place in Westchester and Dorothy Curran's there. Temporarily. It's a kind of way station for the doctor's patients. A place where he can observe them. Nora got the car so that she could drive up to see her sister. And yes, Johnny, it's a green Chevrolet—a dark green Chevy."

"Any idea where she garages it, Bernie?"

"Against a curb," Bernie Simmons said. "As near as she can get to her apartment house. A lot of New York cars live on the streets."

John Stein knew that a lot of New York cars live against curbs, and sometimes get tagged for it and often don't. And that garage rates are high in Manhattan.

"It's not an express street," Bernie said and thought his remark aimless—worried and aimless. Lieutenant John Stein, Homicide North, was not concerned with traffic violations. Unless, of course, they led to violent death—to planned death.

There was plenty of traffic on First Avenue. And at the corner they came to there was a telephone booth. "May as well check in before I call it a night," Stein said, and went into the booth and closed the door after him. He was in the booth for almost five minutes and Simmons waited for him. When Stein came out he shook his head.

"Miss Curran doesn't answer her telephone, Bernie," Stein said. "I let it ring quite a while. If she's there she must be a heavy sleeper. Happen to know whether she is, Bernie?"

"I don't sleep with her," Simmons said. There was exasperation in his voice.

"Don't get steamed up, Bernie," Stein said. "I'm not the morals squad. The boys are going to keep on trying to get her. Maybe, after a while, somebody'll drop around."

"And," Simmons said, "check out the cars parked on the block. Looking for a dark green Chevy."

"Yes, Bernie."

"There's no way she, or anyone, could have known that Fremont was going to see Meade tonight. Meade didn't."

"There's that, Bernie."

"There are thousands of dark green Chevrolets around."

"Yes, Bernie. And we don't know it was a Chevy. Just that it may have been. Miss Pickett—Mrs. Bryan Colley—owns a dark blue Pontiac. It's in the garage under her apartment house. General Motors cars look pretty much alike. The standard sedans, that is."

"Did your man ever catch up with the Shaffner?"

"Not quite," Stein said, and told Bernie why it was not quite.

Rosalie Shaffner had got off the train at Stamford, and Detective Lawrence had got off after her. She had gone through the underpass and got on the one-car train waiting on the New Canaan branch. Lawrence got on it too. Rosalie Shaffner had stayed in the car until it reached New Canaan. "A very swaying ride, Bill Lawrence says. Says he got seasick."

In the station parking lot at New Canaan, Miss Shaffner had picked up a car and driven off in it. There had been nobody in the car; either she had a key for it or the key had been left for her.

"There's a taxi stand at the station," Stein said. "Lawrence got to it just in time to see the only cab drive off. The station there closes at night. He had to walk a couple of blocks before he found a telephone. By the time he got back to the station the one-car train had taken off for Stamford.

"A policeman's lot is not a happy one," Bernie said. "When did the train get to New Canaan?"

"It was due at ten-forty. It got there a little before eleven."

"When Miss Shaffner got off the train," Bernie said. "Went to the lot and picked up this car—her own, or one a friend had left for her or whatever—did she seem in a hurry, did Lawrence say?"

"He didn't say."

"All right," Simmons said. "Was the car she drove off in, at around eleven, a dark green Chevy?"

"No," Stein said. "Coincidence has to stop somewhere, Bernie. It was, as nearly as Lawrence could make out—the light isn't good in the station yard—a dark gray Olds. And yes, Bernie, standard General Motors cars have a family resemblance."

"An hour and maybe fifteen minutes from New Canaan to the upper East Side," Bernie said. "If you know your way and move right along."

"Yes, Bernie. And a couple of technical men are going over and have a look at Meade's car—the one you looked at. Without getting caught at it, if they can manage. And oh, yes, Mr. and Mrs. Simpson do live in New Canaan, Bernie. We got them—him, that is—on the telephone at a little after midnight. Just got home from dinner, he said. And yes, he had told Meade he didn't want the job back. And neither of the cars they own is a dark green Chevy. One's a Volks. The other's a Mercedes. Satisfied, Bernie?"

"Not especially," Bernie Simmons said, and waved down a cab.

"Drop me at a subway station," Stein said.

Simmons dropped him at a Lexington Avenue subway station and kept the cab. He rode home in it, but when it stopped in front of the apartment house and the driver reached toward his flag Bernie said, "Hold it, will you? Put it on waiting time. Five minutes."

"Well," the hacker said, dragging it out.

"All right," Simmons said, "I'll trust you then," and gave the driver a five-dollar bill. He also wrote down the driver's hack number from the posted card and let the driver see him do it. Trust need not be carried to extremes.

The cab was waiting when Bernie came down from his apartment. Bernie gave the driver the address on West End Avenue he had looked up in the Manhattan directory.

"Look, mister," the driver said, "I'm due to check in. The garage is over in Queens, mister."

"No off-duty sign when I hailed you," Simmons said. "Let's go uptown."

"Hell of a note," the hacker said, but he drove uptown.

The apartment house was big. It was also old. A uniformed patrolman stood just outside the entrance, and when Simmons, after telling the taxi driver he could keep what was left over from the five, started to go in the patrolman said, "Hey, you. You live here?"

"No," Simmons said.

"On account of if you're another reporter," the patrolman said, "she doesn't want to see any reporters."

"Miss Fremont?" Simmons said. "No, I'm not a reporter. Been several of them?"

"Woman from the *News*," the patrolman said. "Photographer with her. And a man from the *Times*. Where you from, mister?"

"The District Attorney's office," Simmons said, to which the patrolman said, "Oh. Hear her brother got killed. But what I heard, it was just a traffic accident. You got identification, mister?"

The "mister" was differently inflected this time. The new inflection left a space open for a name. Simmons gave him the name. He gave him identification to go with it. The patrolman said, "Six B, Mr. Simmons," and Bernie went into a cavernous lobby. Probably built some time in the twenties, Bernie thought of the building, and went up in a self-operated elevator and along a corridor, his feet making a grating sound on cement flooring, and pressed a button beside a door lettered "6B." He waited some seconds and pressed it again and heard footfalls inside. The door opened to the extent of a safety chain.

The woman who opened the door was tall and gaunt; she wore her gray hair tightly pulled back into a knob. She said. "Go away. The poor man's dead, they say. Isn't that enough?"

She wore a black dress, which hung loosely on her. She hadn't, Simmons thought, while explaining who he was, been crying.

"It's the middle of the night," she said. "Some drunken hoodlum runs my brother down in a car and kills him. What more do you want?"

"To find out," Simmons said, "if it was only that, Miss Fremont. You are Miss Fremont?"

"Ruth Fremont," she said. "What would I know about it? A man who says he's a detective comes around and says he's sorry to have to tell me Robert's dead and that somebody ran him down over somewhere on the East Side and have I got anybody to stay with me."

"Have you?"

"Why? My poor brother's dead. What can anybody do about that? Hold my hand? I don't need it."

"Miss Fremont," Bernie said, "I don't know what you can tell us that will help us find out who killed your brother. If it wasn't just a drunken driver—or a careless driver. Did the detective who came to see you say the driver was drunk, Miss Fremont? Because we don't know that he was. Or she was."

"Carousing around in cars," she said. "Killing good people. Worthy people. My brother was a man of God, Mr. Simmons. A righteous man."

"I'm sure," Bernie said. "Suppose you let me in and we'll talk about him. And, about this evening. Before—he did come home from the office? And go out again?"

"He didn't tell me where he was going, if that's what you're after. Oh, I guess you can come in."

She released the safety chain and opened the door. As

soon as he was inside she closed it and reset the chain. She led him down a long, straight hallway, with closed doors on either side. The apartment, Bernie thought as he followed her, was almost as cavernous as the lobby. In the early twenties builders still threw space around. As times changed, particularly during the Depression, big apartments were cut up into smaller ones. He thought this one had not been.

She opened a door at the end of the hallway and he followed her into a large square room. It was hot in the room. At the far side of the room heavy curtains, of no special color—he thought of beige—covered windows which evidently were closed. A settee—there was no other word for it—was against one wall and looked, Bernie thought, as if it would resent being sat on. There were several small chairs, armless and with uncompromising backs. In the center of the room there was a round table with a strip of dimly embroidered cloth across it. On the strip, and squared to it, was a Bible. Bernie felt that he had stepped into an uncompromising past.

"Sit down if you want to," Ruth Fremont told him, and herself sat, very upright, on the unyielding settee. Bernie sat on one of the straight chairs, which did not welcome him. Miss Fremont said, "Well?"

If she wanted no nonsense he would give her no nonsense.

"What time, about, did your brother come home this evening?" he asked the black-clad woman who sat with both feet flatly on the floor.

"About eight. There had been some sort of reception at the office. He had felt it his duty to attend. His obligation."

She wanted no nonsense.

"Was he sober when he got here?"

She repeated, "Sober?" with distaste.

"Sober," Bernie said, clarifying it for her.

"Certainly," she said. "What a peculiar question. Robert was abstemious. As became his calling. There is no liquor in this house."

"This reception at the office," Simmons said, using her word for it. "There was a bar. Liquor was served. Was your brother a teetotaler, Miss Fremont?"

"I believe," she said, "that he now and then allowed himself a small glass of sherry. Nothing stronger, certainly."

She wanted no nonsense.

"We've been told," Simmons said, "that your brother, when he was actively a clergyman, lost two parishes because he occasionally drank too much. That isn't true?"

"Evil-doers," the angular woman said. "Spreading malicious rumors against a godly man. My brother left these parishes you speak of because he felt he could best serve the Almighty in another capacity. Because of the frailty of his voice."

It was Bernie's turn to repeat a word with the inflection rising.

"When he delivered his sermons," Miss Fremont said, "they couldn't hear him. Or said they couldn't. I think they did not wish to hear the word of God without compromise. There are many such, Mr. Simmons. Many such in this Godless day and age. This age of carousing. Of open disbelief in the teachings of our Saviour. Are you a Christian, Mr. Simmons?"

"Nominally, at least," Simmons told her. "An Episcopalian, as your brother was. I don't pretend—"

He caught himself before he wandered further from the subject. (He just avoided saying, "Be that as it may," circling a pitfall of the archaic.) He said, "Your brother seemed, then, to be quite normal? I mean, not upset in any way?"

"He looked tired," she said. "And displeased. He found such receptions as this may have been distasteful. You say liquor was served?"

"Yes," Bernie said. "Liquor certainly was served."

"I am surprised," she said, "that Mr. Meade would permit such a thing. My brother always felt that Mr. Meade stood for the higher things."

"He admired Mr. Meade?"

"He felt that Mr. Meade was conscious of the true values

in life. That he sought to have them reflected in the pages of *The Home Guardian*. That by writing for the magazine he —my brother I mean—was serving the Almighty."

Bernie said that that was very commendable. One cannot avoid all pitfalls. He said, "It was that which made him accept the job? The opportunity to serve? Rather than the financial returns?"

(The trouble with me, Bernie thought, is that I take on the idiom of the surroundings. One trouble with me, anyway.)

"Our father," Ruth Fremont said, "left my brother and me well provided for. Financial returns have always been of little importance. One cannot serve God and mammon."

Nice, all the same, to have mammon handy, Bernie thought, and pulled himself back.

"Your brother came home about eight," he said. "Seemed tired and displeased. But perfectly sober. Did he have dinner?"

"He said he had eaten at the reception. He went to his room to rest. And, I imagine, to pray."

"But he went out again. When?"

She thought about ten-thirty. Perhaps nearer eleven. "After he made a telephone call."

"You heard him make a call, Miss Fremont?"

"I was passing his door," she said. "I heard him dialing. In his den."

"But not what he said?"

"I am not one who eavesdrops, Mr. Simmons. In any event, this is a well-constructed building. Not like some of these gimcrack places they put up nowadays. My father would not countenance shoddy workmanship such as is accepted in these days."

"Your father?"

"Certainly. This building was his. He also owned several others. They are my brother's and mine. Now, I suppose, mine."

"So you have no idea whom your brother may have called?"

"Certainly not."

"He went out shortly after he made this call?"

"I told you that."

"And did not say where he was going?"

"No."

"Did he often do that? I mean, go out without saying where or why?"

"Sometimes. I did not intrude on his life."

"Miss Fremont, had your brother ever been married?"

"No. Such things did not enter into his life." Distaste for "such things" was evident in her tone.

"He was younger than you, Miss Fremont?"

"Almost ten years younger."

"And you have shared this apartment for some time?"

"Since we were children. Except when he served in parishes upstate."

"When he did, you went with him?"

"Always. It was my poor way of serving."

"Where your brother was hit by the car," Bernie said, "was quite close to Mr. Meade's house. He didn't say—you didn't guess—he was going there?"

"I've told you I have no idea where he went."

"But if something was, say, troubling him—some special thing—he might go to talk to Mr. Meade? Whom he admired, you say."

"If he had felt it his duty."

"He didn't, when he came home this evening, say anything about having lost his job? Because of a change of management at the magazine?"

"Nothing. Oh, he had mentioned that some broadcasting company had bought an interest in *The Home Guardian*. Had he lost his position?"

"Yes."

"The righteous," Miss Fremont said, "are seldom rewarded in this world."

And that, Bernie thought, seemed as good a place to leave it as any other. Also, he wanted a cigarette and this hot, stuffy room of another time was no place for the flippancy of a cigarette. He might, he suspected, as well have taken a flask out of his pocket as a package of cigarettes. He said he was sorry to have bothered Miss Fremont so late at night, and in an hour of bereavement.

"I sleep little," she said and there was pride in her voice. There is virtue in abstention from comfort. Sleep is for the slothful, who are likewise the ungodly.

She followed him down the long hall. "Which was your brother's room?" he asked her, and she pointed toward one of the closed doors.

"It is locked," she said. "He always locked it when he left. I do not intend that his documents shall be disturbed."

The room would be gone over, whatever her intentions might be. He did not raise the issue. There would be time for that. He said, "Your room?"

Her room was across the hall from her brother's.

"An extension telephone in his room," Bernie said. "In yours, Miss Fremont?"

"Certainly not," she said. "The only telephone in the apartment is in my brother's room."

There is virtue, also, in avoiding convenience.

She locked the apartment door after him and he could hear through it the clink of the safety chain into its socket.

On the sidewalk in front of the big old building Bernie Simmons had ample time, while he waited for a taxi, to try to pull things together. They did not pull.

Fremont had telephoned somebody and then gone out, and gone out between ten-thirty and eleven. He had been sober. He had showed up at Meade's house around midnight and showed up unexpectedly. Therefore, if everybody was telling the truth, it was not Meade he had telephoned before he left—without telling his sister where he was going. Which was puzzling; Bernie would have expected the dour, evangelical woman to ride herd on her younger brother.

Between the time he left the building on West End Avenue and the time he got to Meade's narrow house near the East River, Fremont would have had ample time to stop for drinks. (Unless he had spent most of it waiting for a taxicab, as began to Bernie Simmons to seem entirely possible.) Had a few to nerve himself to appeal to Meade for his job—almost to grovel for it? But, a job he did not financially need. Unless, conceivably, his sister held the purse strings and held them tightly.

Not the money, the salary *The Guardian* paid him? Something less tangible, as Meade himself had thought possible. The need of the job as an assurance of personal identity. How had Meade phrased it? Lost himself without the job. Oh, yes—"the shape of himself."

Called somebody and asked whoever it was to meet him at Meade's house? But nobody else had showed up there, according to Meade. In the house, at any rate. Somebody had met Fremont outside the house, harshly and fatally. Somebody who had known he was going there?

You pulled and pulled and it didn't pull together. Also, he couldn't make his mind grip it fully. His mind kept drifting away—kept drifting in search of a slim, brown-haired girl named Nora Curran; a girl who did not answer the telephone in her apartment, late at night.

Two blocks away, Bernie saw a cab with its roof lights on. He stepped out into the wide street and waved both arms at it. When he was nearer, he saw that the roof lights spelled "Off Duty." But when it was a block away, the lights changed to spell out "Taxi." Which meant that Bernie Simmons looked like an acceptable fare.

The cab pulled up and the driver said, "Which way, mister?"

Bernie got into the cab before he answered and the hacker turned and glowered at him. "I was off duty," the hacker said. "I was trying to do you a favor, mister, if you're going downtown."

"Downtown," Bernie said, and gave him the address in the East Fifties.

The driver said, "O.K., mister," and took him there. It was well after one-thirty in the morning when Bernie lifted the telephone from the cradle and spun the dial.

XI

The Police Department of the City of New York does not sleep, although its members do not, by and large, think of insomnia as a virtue. (Lieutenant John Stein was almost certainly sleeping peacefully in his apartment in Brooklyn; Detective Paul Lane was beyond doubt home and in bed.)

Bernie had to speak to several detectives, and finally to the lieutenant on night duty at Homicide, Manhattan North, before he got what he wanted.

The technical men, during a cursory examination, had found nothing to indicate that Meade's big Cadillac had recently run into anything. They had found three green Chevrolets parked in the block Nora Curran lived in, and two of them had dents in right front fenders. They had taken the license numbers of the dented cars and of the other Chevy. In the morning, if things were not cleared up by morning, the slow checkout of companies which leased cars would begin. There was no point in starting what might be a tedious investigation in the middle of the night. Business offices do sleep.

There was a preliminary report from the medical examiner's office. Fremont had died of a crushed skull. There was a bruise on his left hip, as if he had been struck a glancing blow.

"According to a witness," Simmons said, "Fremont staggered off the sidewalk into the street and a car hit him and threw him across the sidewalk and up against a building. Head first, and maybe into—oh, a stone step. That would fit with what the M.E.'s office says?"

It would.

"Impact like that, I mean between the car and the man's

body, wouldn't necessarily dent the car? Or scratch the paint?"

The lieutenant wouldn't think so. That would be up to the lab boys. "When we find the car, if we ever find the car."

I ought to call it a night, Bernie thought. I'm being a cop again, and I'm not a cop. Johnny Stein's right. I ought to let the cops do the nosing around; let them bring me the evidence for decision as to whether it justifies a charge. It's late as hell to call Nora.

He called Nora. The telephone in her apartment rang twice and she said, "Hello." She did not sound sleepy. He said, "Sorry, dear. I do know what time it is." She said, "Yes, Bernie, I'm sure you do."

"All right," Bernie said, "where have you been all night, girl? Out carousing?"

She laughed at that. She said, "What a word, Bernie. I don't carouse."

"Where?" Bernie said. "And wherever it was, in your car? It could be important, Nora."

Briefly, he told her why it might be important.

"The poor man," Nora said. "The poor little man."

"At the party," Bernie said. "You saw him at the party?"

"Once or twice. I think once or twice. It was a big party—and poor Mr. Fremont was the kind who—who tends to disappear in big parties. You know the kind I mean, Bernie?"

"Yes. Did you happen to notice whether he was drinking? I mean, drinking a lot?"

"No. But in the elevator he didn't look as if he were drunk. Just—sort of dazed. He didn't stagger or anything."

"In the elevator? When was that?"

"When I was leaving. Almost everybody else had already left, I think."

She told him about riding down with Fremont in the elevator.

"He looked—what did you say—dazed?"

"Blank. Yes—dazed. But I was a bit dazed myself, Bernie. Perhaps—it's like when you've had a drink too many. Sometimes, when you're that way, you think it's other people who've been drinking too much. Perhaps I was the one who was dazed. More than poor Rev-rob."

"Dazed," Bernie said. "Not—oh, jittery? Frightened?"

"As if he had just killed somebody? I don't know how a person would look if he had just killed somebody. Bernie, he wouldn't. He—oh, he was rather like a rabbit. Rabbits don't kill."

You can't, he told her, tell who will kill. He did, in general, agree about rabbits.

"Anyway," she said, "Somebody killed *him*. Unless it was just an accident."

"Or," Bernie said, "unless he saw the car coming and jumped in front of it. To expiate. A life for a life."

"Do you believe that? At all believe that?"

"I don't at the moment know what I believe," Bernie told her. "Remorse. A sense of sin which demanded atonement. He was a very religious man, apparently. At least his sister thought he was. And, I gathered—his sister is an odd one—he thought *The Guardian* was—call it a bulwark against evil-doers. A dike holding back the unrighteous. With Meade's finger in it."

"Bernie? For heaven's sake!"

"What it came to," Bernie said. "At least I gathered she thought that. She, however, is fanatical. Or seems to be. Perhaps she laid it on a bit thick. To get back, dear. Where were you tonight? After Stein and I left? And, were you in the car?"

"I got a telephone call from Dr. Werke's nurse," she said. "She told me—"

The nurse had told Nora that her sister, who was supposed to be safe in the doctor's interim sanitarium in Westchester County, had somehow managed to get out of it. There was supervision; nobody knew precisely how the supervision had failed.

"We're so very careful," the nurse told Nora. "It's never happened before."

What had happened was that Dorothy Curran was safely

in her bedroom, apparently asleep, at a little before ten. At a quarter after ten she was not. She was wearing a nightgown; presumably a robe over it. Almost certainly, she was still somewhere on the grounds. They were looking for her. They had no doubt they would find her, and Nora was not to worry at all. Not at all.

"Idiotic of them to call you," Bernie Simmons said.

"Oh, I wanted them to. And—there's a little lake on the grounds, Bernie. The very pretty grounds around Dr. Werke's house. It's—it's where they would look first, Bernie."

"They asked you to go up and help look for her?"

They had not. They had told her they were sure everything would be all right.

"Sometimes," Nora said, "I can get through to her when nobody else can."

She had got the car from its parking place across the street. She had driven across town and up the West Side Highway and on. Near the beginning of the Saw Mill River Parkway she had stopped at a filling station and telephoned ahead—and got good news. While most of the staff was searching the grounds for her, Dorothy Curran had returned to the house, and to her room and to bed. They had found her sleeping in her bed. The slippers she had worn were soaking wet with dew.

Nora had driven on to the nearest exit from the Parkway and, after a little wandering on unknown roads, found her way back onto it, heading south. She had got home about half an hour before Bernie called.

"Nora," Bernie said, "is there a dent in this car you've got on lease? And, it is a green Chevrolet."

It was. She had never noticed any special dents. Where?

"Right front fender, probably," Bernie said.

She said, "Oh," and then for seconds nothing further. Finally, in a voice which shook a little, she said, "You think that, Bernie?"

"No," he said. "I don't think that, darling."

"Lieutenant Stein does?"

"That it's a possibility, I suppose. The car which hit Fremont was probably a green Chevy. At least, Meade thinks it may have been. Nora, did you ever drive to the office in the car? Park it near the building?"

"Once or twice, I think. When I went back after dinner to finish up. Never in the daytime. There's never any place to park. I take—have always taken—a taxi when I could get one. Otherwise, I walk. It's only half a dozen blocks."

Did she know the license number of the leased car?

She could look it up. She was gone minutes. She said, "It's—" and gave him the number.

Where had she parked the car?

"Almost directly across the street," she said. "I—wait a minute, Bernie."

He waited less than a minute.

"I looked out the window," Nora said. "It's there, Bernie. I'm afraid it's a little too near a fire hydrant, but it's there. Will I get a ticket on top of everything else?"

The lightness in her voice was forced, Bernie thought.

"If you do," he said, "I'll get it fixed." Which was rather a rash promise. "Go to bed, darling. Take a sleeping pill and go to bed. That's what I'm going to do. Promise?"

"I guess so," Nora Curran said. "I don't think it will do any good. But I guess so, Bernie. Good night, Bernie."

"Everything will be all right."

"Of course, Bernie. Good night, Bernie."

She hung up, then. After several seconds, with a feeling of great reluctance, Bernie Simmons cradled his own telephone.

He did not take a sleeping pill and go to sleep. He went out and walked the few blocks which separated his apartment house from the one Nora lived in.

The green Chevrolet was where she had said it would be. He crouched down by it and looked at the right front fender. The light was dim; he should, he thought, have brought a flashlight. He ran a hand over the gritty smoothness of the fender. There seemed to be a dent. Not a big dent. She would have a flashlight in the glove compartment, probably. He tried the car door. The door was locked.

There was the sound of a door opening across the street and he turned and faced across the street. Nora, in dark slacks and a dark blouse, was crossing the sidewalk. She had a flashlight in her hand. She gave it to him.

"I wasn't sleepy," Nora said. "Anyway, you sounded as if you might come."

Together, shoulders touching, they crouched beside the green Chevrolet.

There was a dent, all right. It was not a big dent. The paint surface was not broken. It might have been made when the car brushed, lightly, against something. It might have been made when another car, worrying its way out of a tight parking space, had backed into it.

"I'm trying to do a technician's work," Bernie said, when they stood up. He put an arm around her shoulders. "A policeman's work."

"Yes, dear," Nora said. "You have before, haven't you? What are you going to do now?"

"See you to your apartment door," Bernie said. "Kiss you gently on the forehead. See that you go into your apartment and lock the door after you."

"Then?"

"Go home myself and—" But he did not finish that. He merely for some seconds stood, holding her to him, and looking over her head at nothing in particular.

"Or perhaps," Bernie said, "go over to the *Guardian* office and listen to a tape recording. If I can make it work."

"I," Nora said, "am quite familiar with tape recorders."

They drove over in the green Chevrolet. At two o'clock in the morning there was no special difficulty in finding a place to park. Many of the windows on the many floors of the tall office building had lights behind them. It was still an hour for cleaning women; it was still, conceivably, an hour for late office workers.

The lobby was brightly lighted. The air in it was fresh and cool. The newsstand-cigar counter was shuttered and padlocked. A uniformed guard looked at them but did nothing to stop them. Apparently they passed muster; probably his chief duty was to prevent vagrants from using the lobby as a dormitory. The doors of two of the express elevators stood open and when, in one of them, Bernie Simmons pressed the button numbered "37," the doors closed and the car shot up.

The elevator lobby on the thirty-seventh floor was as brightly lighted as the lower lobby. The double glass doors lettered "The Home Guardian" were locked. A uniformed patrolman—who had been sitting down and smoking a cigarette on the other side of the doors—got up rather hurriedly and stepped on the cigarette. He came to the glass doors and looked at them, and shook his head. It is difficult to establish identity through thick glass doors. Bernie tried it by voice and the patrolman kept on shaking his head. Bernie got his official identification card out of his wallet and pressed it against the glass and the patrolman continued to shake his head. He did, however, come to the door and read through the glass. Then he went away, out of sight. He came back with another patrolman, who was also shaking his head. The second patrolman read the identification card through the glass. They conferred, soundlessly to the two outside. Then one of them opened one of the glass doors.

"Orders are nobody," the one who had opened the doors said. "Let's see that card again."

Bernie let him see the card again. He added voice to it. "It says, assistant district attorney," Bernie told the cop. "It says, Bernard Simmons. I'm cooperating with Lieutenant Stein."

The two patrolmen looked at each other. "Orders are nobody," one of them said. "Guess it's all right for Mr. Simmons," the other said. "Heard about him, seems like. Who's the lady, Mr. Simmons?"

Bernie told them who the lady was.

"Guess it's all right," the one who had stood firmly to orders said, and Bernie Simmons and Nora Curran went into the reception office of *The Guardian*. There were doors on either side of the room, and at the rear of it. They stood open.

"It's strange at night," Nora said, as they walked across the reception office. "Empty. Different. There are always so many people."

It was even stranger in the big general office, so regimented by many empty desks, and not so brightly lighted.

"It's somehow like walking through a cemetery," Nora said, as they walked through it. "As if the desks were tombstones."

Beyond the general office, the corridor from which the main offices opened was dimly lighted.

"Over here, I think," Nora said, and went a little way down the corridor and found light switches. One of them, pressed on, turned on overhead lights.

The doors to the office Bryan Colley had died in and to Meade's corner office both were closed. Bernie turned the knob of the nearest, which was the one Colley had taken over from a man named Nelson Barclay. He pushed and the door opened silently.

He stopped pushing when the door was barely ajar and pulled it to again. He said, "Listen, Nora," and turned the knob again. He said, "Hear anything?"

"Barely," she said. "A little click."

He tried it several more times, the last time bending down so that an ear was very close to the lock. The click of the latch tongue parting from the striking plate still was only barely perceptible.

He went into the office, saying "When I tell you" to Nora Curran, and closed the door behind him. After a few seconds he said, "O.K.," and she turned the knob and opened the door and went into the office.

Bernie Simmons was sitting behind the desk Colley had collapsed on to die.

He said, "Yes, I could hear it. Just hear it. It's a well-installed lock, apparently. And, apparently, the tape recorder has better ears than mine."

He got up from behind the desk and brushed his hands together, brushing fingerprint dust off them. Nora said, "The other door, Bernie?"

But he was already crossing the room toward the door between this office and the big corner office next to it. The door probably would be locked again, he thought. Probably Paul Lane had used his gimmick to re-lock a door he had unlocked with it. Bernie turned the knob and the latch clicked and the door opened. The click of this lock was not loud, but it was distinct.

The only light in Meade's office came through the door they had opened. It took a little groping to find a light switch, and while Bernie groped Nora stood in the doorway and her breathing quickened. But when the lights went on, the room was empty. She let stored breath out in a sigh.

"Yes," Bernie said, "I was too, a little."

Again, as he had with the other door, Bernie opened several times and closed several times the interconnecting door. Each time the latch clicked. The door which opened from this office to the corridor also clicked, but not so loudly.

"Probably," Bernie said, "it depends on how precisely the locks and striking plates are matched up when the doors are installed. A fraction of an inch would make a good bit of difference, I'd think. Only, I don't really know anything about locks."

He turned back from the door he had been testing and looked across the room, apparently at nothing. Then he looked at Nora.

"Except," he said, "that there are always two keys for every lock. At least, I think there are."

"There are two keys to my apartment," Nora said. "I remember that when I first moved in there were two keys. I don't know what happened to the one I don't use. I suppose it's in a drawer some place."

Unexpectedly, Bernie grinned at her. "Unless, of course, you gave it to a boy friend."

She was very grave when she answered and said, "I really can't remember that I ever did, Bernie. I'm almost sure it's in a drawer some place."

"I hope so," Bernie said, and his voice, also, was grave. "I really do hope so, girl."

And then they both laughed, for no very obvious reason. The laughter was brief.

"Putting a spare key in a drawer somewhere is, at a guess, almost a reflex with most people," Bernie said, and spoke slowly. "In my desk at home there's a drawer with—oh, half a dozen keys in it. I suppose the second key to the apartment is one of them. I haven't, offhand, any idea what the other keys open. Luggage keys, perhaps. Do you lock luggage when you're going places, Nora?"

"I always think I ought to," Nora said. "It's such a prudent, orderly thing to do. But I guess I don't, Bernie. Or, know where the keys are."

"Meade," Bernie said, "seems quite sure there is only one key to the interconnecting door. And that the lock on the corridor door works with the same key. And that, tonight, he had that only key in his pocket."

"Perhaps," she said, "he lost the other. And—perhaps, Bernie, somebody else found it. And hung onto it."

"Foresighted of somebody," Bernie said. "Let's look in some drawers, dear. Probably already been done, but still— Meade may have put the other key somewhere—his desk would be a likely place—and forgotten he did."

"The desk," Nora said, "probably is locked up tight. Mr. Meade is an orderly man, from what little I know of him. A precise, careful man. He looks it, doesn't he? At the office always the same gray suit. I don't mean the same one. Probably he had them made four or five at a time."

They might as well see whether Meade's orderliness extended to the locking up of an office desk. They went, together, behind the desk—a flat-top desk, heavy like the other furniture in the room. There was a center drawer and three drawers on each side. The center drawer was not locked. There were note pads in it and several pencils, all extremely pointed, and a checkbook with "Jefferson Meade" printed on in gilt. There was a box of paper clips and a framed roll of adhesive tape. There was also a typed manuscript, in carbon copy. There were pencil notations on the top page of the manuscript.

"Always they send us carbons," Nora said. "They smudge off on your hands. Of book-length manuscripts, I mean. After they send the ribbon copies to book publishers. I'm talking too much. I do, I guess, when I'm knotted up."

"Everybody does," Bernie told her. "Or else doesn't say anything at all."

He shuffled long-fingered hands through the desk drawer. There wasn't any key.

They crouched on either side of the desk and worked down through the other drawers. None of them was locked. There was a miscellany of papers in the top drawer on Nora's side. There were contract forms with many blank spaces in them; there was a short manuscript which, she recognized, had been finished with by one of the copy-editors and now was ready for Meade's final approval. She lifted the papers out and shook them and no key fell out from between sheets of paper. She went down to the next drawer.

"Nothing in this one," Bernie said and closed the top drawer on his side. "That is, a lot of stuff but no key."

He opened the drawer below.

It was Nora who found the key—found a key. It was in a bottom drawer, under several copies of past issues of *The Guardian* and a clipped-together sheaf of newspaper clippings. The uppermost clippings concerned the purchase by the United Broadcasting Network of a controlling interest in *The Home Guardian*, more generally known simply as *The Guardian*.

A key was under everything in the far right-hand corner of the drawer. It was by itself there.

Nora fished it out and stood up, holding the key flat between thumb and forefinger. She said, "Could this be it, Bernie?" and held it toward him. And Bernie Simmons said, "Oops, darling!"

"The wrong key?" she said. "Is that the oops, Bernie?"

"The oops," Bernie said, "is for what Johnny Stein will think of us. Fingerprints, girl. Policemen are very fond of fingerprints." He reached out for the key. "Fonder, on the whole, than juries," Bernie said, and took the key from her. He held it as she had held it; he moved it between his fingers, rubbing it between them.

"Since the harm's done," Bernie said, "we may as well see it's thoroughly done. What's worth doing at all. Yes, it looks like the same kind of key."

The key fitted smoothly into the keyhole of the door between the two offices. It worked as smoothly, turned as readily, in the lock of the door which opened on the corridor.

"So anybody, with time enough to look through the desk, could have found it," Nora said. "At any time Mr. Meade wasn't in the office. While he was making his speech at the start of the party. When he was talking to people at the party afterward. Put it in a pocket. Or put it in a handbag, of course. To use after Mr. Meade had locked up."

"And put it back. Why put it back, Nora? Why not just keep it? Or, throw it away? Drop it down a sidewalk grating?"

She said, "Oh." Then she said, "I don't know, Bernie. Unless whoever it was thought the police would search everybody."

"No," he said. "There was plenty of time to get rid of the key before the police showed up. Before the cleaning woman found Colley's body. Why put it back for us to find?"

He looked at the key he still held, as if, somehow, it were more than a key. It kept on being a key, however hard he looked at it.

"I don't know," Nora said. "Perhaps—"

The sound of a latch click interrupted her. They both turned to face the door which led to the corridor. And Nora Curran shrank back a little toward the tall, red-haired man.

The door opened and there was nothing surreptitious about the method of its opening. It opened and a man as tall as the man Nora shrank back against stood in the doorway. This man had gray hair.

"Well," Jefferson Meade said, "and what are you two doing in my office?"

He spoke pleasantly. There was no hostility in his tone. There was, as far as Bernie Simmons could tell, merely natural curiosity.

"I came to hear that tape recording again," Simmons said. "Miss Curran came to help me run the thing. And you, Mr. Meade? To put in a little overtime?"

"Precisely," Meade said, and came on into his office and closed the door after him. "Or, at least very largely. Can I offer you two a drink?"

Neither of them wanted a drink. "I do," Meade said, and went into the room off the office which was bathroom, dressing room and, apparently, bar. They heard him break ice cubes out of a tray and then heard a thumping sound. Then he came back with a tall glass filled with a brownish milky liquid. He sat down at his desk and put the glass down in front of him.

He was not wearing the gray suit Nora had said he always seemed to wear. He wore dark slacks and a pull-over sports shirt of dark blue.

"Didn't expect to run into anybody," he said. "Spur-of-the-moment decision, after I'd gone to bed and found I couldn't sleep. Things kept going over and over in my mind. Nagging things."

"To do with getting out the magazine? Now you're editing it again?"

"That," Meade said. "Very much that. Especially—"

He opened the top drawer of his desk and took out the thick manuscript in it.

"This," he said, and put the manuscript on top of the desk. "I've been mulling over it for days. It's almost right but it doesn't—oh, doesn't feel quite right. When I couldn't sleep I got to thinking about this piece and got an idea what could be done with it. What we can use of it."

"And came down in the middle of the night—after the middle of the night—to read the manuscript and see if you were right?"

"Seems unlikely to you, Mr. Simmons? Actually, to take it home and go over it during the weekend."

He looked suddenly at Nora Curran and smiled at her.

"I'd wager," he said, "that it doesn't seem odd to you, Miss Curran. You take your work home with you sometimes,

I'm sure. Whether you want to or not. Not always physically. But at least in your mind?"

"Yes," she said, and turned to Bernie. "It's part of editing stories, Bernie. And, deciding about them. Whether to send them on up with a recommendation. Or just to send them back with a polite note. And for Mr. Meade it's—oh, it must be infinitely more a pressure. I just have suggestions, of course. He has decisions."

"You are a knowledgeable young woman, Miss Curran," Meade said. "Good decisions or bad decisions, I have to make them. For now, any way. As long as *The Guardian*'s still mine to edit."

"Understandable," Bernie said. "I often take cases home with me between court sessions. And worry them at nights. What else brought you here tonight, Mr. Meade?"

XII

The question appeared to puzzle Meade. He looked at Bernie Simmons and raised carefully trimmed gray eyebrows and shook his head.

"When you came in," Bernie said, "I asked if you'd come to do some overtime. You said, 'Precisely.' But then you added, 'Or at least very largely.' I took that to mean you had a second reason for coming to the office at this time of night."

"Of course," Meade said. "Finding you two here put it out of my mind. I came to look for another key."

Nora started to speak. Bernie spoke first. He said merely, "Another key, Mr. Meade?"

"All sorts of things churn around in your mind when you can't sleep," Meade said. "I got to wondering about a second key. I'd told you there was only one—you and Lieutenant Stein. That the only one to the two doors to this office was in my pocket. I showed it to you."

"Yes," Bernie said. "You were quite convinced there wasn't another key."

"I got to wondering," Meade said. "You see—"

It had occurred to him, as it had to Bernie, that there are two keys to every lock. It had occurred to him, as thoughts shifted and turned in his sleepless mind, that there must have been, originally, at least two keys to the duplicate locks of the doors to his office. He had tried to remember. He came up, dimly, with the feeling that there had once been two keys.

"It was all very vague," Meade said. "It would have been

several years ago, of course. When we moved in here from the downtown building. It seemed to me that there were two keys then and that I had done something with one of them. Put it some place."

He had got up and gone from his bedroom to his office in the narrow house and looked in his desk there for the second key.

"I felt," Meade told them, "as if I had had two keys and put one of them in a drawer somewhere."

He had searched the desk at home carefully and found no second key. That was, he had found several keys, including one to his safe deposit box. But none of them was the right key. He had his own to compare them with. Then he thought of the desk in the office. He decided to have a look there. "Here."

"As much to get the key as to pick up this manuscript you were worrying about, Mr. Meade?"

"No," Meade said. "The script was the important thing. It seemed suddenly important to compare it with what was in my mind. The key was incidental. As long as I was coming here anyway, I thought I'd have a look for the key."

"You felt the key might be important?"

Meade smiled. There was something rather like forgiveness in his smile.

"Mr. Simmons," he said, "I'm not really a stupid man. Not altogether stupid. You and the lieutenant seemed to think that somebody might have gone from this office to the one next to it. To kill poor Colley. And I'd been insistent that that was impossible, because I had locked the connecting door when I left long before somebody killed Colley. Impossible because I had the only key. You see, Mr. Simmons, I can put two and two together. If there was a second key, here perhaps, it might mean that somebody had found it. And used it. Which would give you—call it an alternative. You agree, Mr. Simmons?"

Simmons did. He also thought that Meade seemed casually amused at the idea he need free himself from any suspicion. Bernie Simmons said he did agree.

"While the party was going on," he said. "Was this office unlocked? So that somebody could have come in and found the key?"

"Certainly," Meade said. "As I remember it, the door was open. The door to the corridor, I mean. Not, as I recall it, the door to the office Colley was using. But I can't be sure about that. I remember—wait. It was open too."

It was open because Colley had come into the corner office before the two of them went to join the party. He had left the door between the offices open.

"We discussed my little pep talk to the staff for a few minutes," Meade said. "Then we went out through this office to the library. Where the party was being held."

"You stayed on at the party after what you call your 'pep talk?'"

"For a time. Half an hour. Perhaps more than that. Doing what I felt to be my duty. But I told you that earlier, didn't I?"

"You told Lieutenant Stein," Bernie said. "Half an hour or more. With your office open for anybody who wanted to go through it to Colley's office and turn on the tape recorder. Need to be somebody who knew Colley was going to call people into his office and fire them. Who'd know about that?"

"I did," Meade said. "Certainly Colley's secretary—this Miss—" He paused. Bernie gave him the name. "Of course," Meade said. "And she may have mentioned to almost anyone that Colley was going to want a few words with him later on. Or Colley may have himself. And—things spread around, you know. Particularly among people who are already edgy."

He pulled open the top drawer of his desk and bent over and began to look into it.

"No," Bernie Simmons said. "Oh, you were right about there being another key. About your having put the spare in a drawer somewhere. It wasn't that drawer, Mr. Meade. The bottom right-hand drawer was where Miss Curran found it."

He took the key out of the pocket he had put it in when Meade first came into the room. He showed Meade the second key.

153

"You mean," Meade said, "somebody found it and used it and then put it back in the desk?"

That, Bernie told him, was the way it looked.

"Some friend of mine, Counselor? Somebody who wanted to provide an alternative?"

"Possibly."

"In that case," Meade said, "I'm in debt to a murderer, aren't I?"

It could be put that way, Bernie agreed. And then somebody knocked heavily on the corridor door to Meade's office.

Meade looked at Bernie Simmons and raised his eyebrows and, slightly, his wide square shoulders. Bernie shook his head. It was Meade who, his voice a little raised, said "Come in."

The door opened and a uniformed patrolman stood in the doorway and looked at them. He looked at them, Bernie thought, with irritation. He looked like a cop who was about to say, "All right, break it up. *Break it up.*"

What he did say was, "How many ways are there into this damn place?" He looked at Jefferson Meade, with irritation and challenge in his narrowed eyes.

"Several, Officer," Meade said. "The main doors, of course. Down the corridor a ways there is a private door. With 'No Admittance' lettered on it. It is also possible to go through the business offices downstairs and come up either by the stairway or in the private elevator. You're wondering how I got in?"

"All right. How did you get in? And, come to that, who are you?"

Meade told the patrolman who he was. He said he had come in through the private entrance, as he usually did. He said, "No surreptitious entry, officer. I used my key."

The patrolman looked thoughtfully at the three of them for a moment. Then he turned and spoke over his shoulder. He said, "All right, Joe. Bring him in," and stepped aside to make that possible.

Again the spindly little man with the too large head had a policeman's hand on each of his narrow shoulders. In the doorway, he shook his shoulders out from under the hands. He turned and looked up at the tall policeman who had held him. He said, "Brutality. That's what it is." The policeman did not say anything. Dr. Clifford Armstrong advanced into the room—more or less skipped into the room. He skipped to Meade's desk and stared at Meade. He said, "What the hell goes on here?"

"Found him in one of the offices," one of the patrolmen said. "Had the door part way open and the lights on. Had a box of papers he was going through. Sort of pawing through. Nobody's supposed to be in here until they come back tomorrow. The place is a goddamn sieve. Excuse it, lady."

"It does seem to be," Simmons said. "Didn't anybody tell you there are several ways in?"

"Nope. Just not to let anybody in. That's all the sergeant said. Nothing about a private door. Or coming up from the floor below."

"All right," Bernie said. "Better split up and cover both doors, hadn't you? I'll talk to Professor Armstrong."

The patrolman who had knocked at the door said, "We-ell," drawing it out.

"Yes," Bernie said. "Go watch the doors. And close that one as you go."

The policeman said, "We-ell," again, drawing it out again. But he backed out of the door and closed it after him.

"Well, Professor?" Bernie Simmons said.

Armstrong did not pay any attention to him. He took a folded paper out of his pocket and unfolded it and slapped it down, flat, on Meade's desk. He said, "All right, Jeff. There it is. Good as a contract, wouldn't you say?"

Meade picked the paper up and looked at it briefly and folded it again and handed it back to the little man who was wagging a big head at him.

"I told you my word was that," Meade said. "Don't fidget so much, Cliff."

"As long as you had the say, I don't doubt it," Armstrong said. "With that son of a bitch Colley moving in— This is black and white, isn't it? On the letterhead. With 'Editor in Chief' under your name."

"We're not trying to welsh," Meade said.

"Suppose," Simmons said mildly, "one of you gentlemen tells me what this paper is. It'll be a place to start."

Armstrong turned abruptly to face Simmons, who thought that such sudden movements might well impair the stability of the professor's big head. Armstrong said, "Who the hell are you? Oh."

"Yes," Simmons said. "We talked a bit earlier. What's that you've brought Mr. Meade, Professor? The letter giving his approval of this piece you're writing for the magazine?"

"You," Armstrong said, "are damned right. Here."

He handed the letter to Simmons and Simmons unfolded it and read:

"Dear Cliff: The script is going along splendidly. It's precisely what I hoped and knew it would be. There may be a few places here and there we'll want to cut a little and we'll go over those things together later on. But the general shape is fine. Get on with it and give me, when you can, your estimate of when you may be finished. Six months or so would work out well with us."

It was signed as Armstrong had said it was signed. It might very well be as good as a contract. Bernie gave it back to the little man who was wagging a big head at him.

"I gather, Professor," Bernie said, "that you found the papers you say had been taken from your office. We're going through them, looking for this letter, I suppose, when the patrolman picked you up."

"I was in my own office. I used my own key to get in here. Do you people think you can push me around?"

"Nobody's pushing," Simmons told him. "As Mr. Meade says, don't fidget so. The key to—"

"Dr. Armstrong has a key to what we all call the back door," Meade said. "He frequently uses his office at nights when the main doors are locked."

"As I have every right to do," Armstrong said. "The office is assigned to me. And nobody had any right to steal my papers out of it. And—"

"All right," Simmons said. "Where did you find these papers of yours, Professor? And—when?"

"Is it any of your—" Armstrong said, and Bernie, who was slightly tired of the historian's fidgets, did not let him finish.

"Yes," Bernie said. "It is my business. You found the papers. Including this letter which, after Colley told you *The Guardian* wasn't going to publish, you very much wanted. Where? Suppose you tell us about it? And it is my business, Professor. Business of mine and the Police Department's."

Nora looked at the red-haired man. She had never before heard this note in his usually quiet voice.

The tone of Bernie Simmons's voice penetrated Clifford Armstrong's fidgets. Armstrong went to one of the deep chairs and sat in it. He more or less disappeared in it, but his strong, heavy voice came out of its depths.

The jumpy little professor of history could be succinct when he wanted to be succinct.

He had gone home after "you were through with me" and had gone to bed. But he, too, found he could not sleep. The importance of the letter Meade had written him grew in his sleepless mind. Finding the letter became something he could not put off. He had got up and looked for the letter in his house and the longer he looked without success the more urgent the need to find it became. Finally, he told them, that urgency came to fill his mind.

He dressed and took the subway from his house in Queens and walked from the subway station to the Park Avenue building. He had used his key to the back door. He had found Percy Winnick's office unlocked and searched in it and, finally, found a ring of keys he had failed to find earlier. They were not tagged for identification, and it was a matter of trial and error before he found the one which fitted the room in which office supplies were stored. And in that room, near the door, he found a carton with his papers in it.

"Thrown in any old way," Armstrong said. "As if it all was waste paper."

The splutter came back into his voice as he said that.

He had taken the carton to his office and taken the papers out—"all higgledy-piggledy they were"—until he found the letter. He had just put it in his pocket and was about to leave when the policeman found him.

"And that's all there was to it," Armstrong said. "And I had every right to look for what was mine."

"You didn't see or hear anyone else in the offices? While you were finding the keys, trying them on the storeroom door until one fitted?"

"No."

"Mr. Winnick's office. The storeroom. Your own office. Those were the only places you went, Professor?"

"Yes."

"Not here?"

"Certainly not. Why would I? Anyway, I knew Mr. Meade always locked his office up when he left for the day." He came partly out of the deep chair so that he could look across Meade's desk at Meade. "You told me that once, didn't you, Jeff?" he said. "I've forgotten how you happened to tell me, but you did."

"Probably," Meade said. "There wasn't any secret about it. Probably everybody on the staff knew I always locked up at the end of the day."

Armstrong popped out of the chair and waggled his head at Bernie Simmons. He said, "Satisfied now?"

"For now," Bernie said. "You can go back home, Professor."

"After I sort out my papers," Armstrong said. "They're every which way."

"Come back tomorrow—later today, that is—and sort your papers," Bernie told him. "Take your letter and go home and get your sleep, Doctor."

"You can't push—"

"Go home," Bernie said. "Go home and quit fidgeting."

Armstrong patted the jacket pocket he had put his letter in. Paper crackled faintly. Not satisfied, Armstrong took the paper out of the pocket and opened it and read it and, precariously, nodded his head at it. Then, rather to Bernie Simmons's surprise, he went out of the office. Bernie followed him and looked down the corridor toward the doors which opened into the general office. One of the patrolmen was standing there.

"Professor Armstrong is leaving," Simmons told the patrolman. "See that he gets out all right, will you?"

The patrolman said, "Come on, Professor," and Armstrong went on, seeming again to skip.

"Odd little man," Meade said, when Bernie was back in the office. "Excitable. But a very fine mind."

"I'm sure," Bernie said. "Mr. Meade, how many people have keys to this back door of yours?"

"Everybody with executive positions," Meade said. "It's a great convenience, sometimes, not to have to go through the reception room."

"People like Miss Shaffner? Mr. Simpson?"

"Certainly, Mr. Simmons."

"Mr. Stubbs?"

"Certainly not. Nobody in the business department. If any of them has occasion to come to the editorial floor, he goes through the reception room, like everybody who doesn't belong here."

"Mr. Colley had one, I assume," Bernie said. "Do you know whether Miss Pickett has?"

"I shouldn't think so. Winnick will know."

"Speaking of Mr. Winnick," Bernie said. "Does he have, with his other keys, one that would fit the doors to this office?"

"No. He does not."

"The only two, then, the one you have in your pocket and the one I, for the time being, have in mine?"

"Yes," Meade said. "And I'm glad you found it, Mr. Simmons. A—shall we say a weight off my mind? Since, as I boasted earlier, I'm not an especially stupid man."

"Oh," Bernie said, "I never supposed you were, Mr. Meade."

"Unless you have more questions?" Meade said, and, when Bernie shook his head, Meade stood up behind his desk. He opened the top drawer and took out of it the manuscript he had come to get. He said, "Then," and came around from behind the desk, tall and erect in his dark slacks and shirt. He said, "Good night, Miss Curran, Mr. Simmons," and opened the door to the corridor. He took keys out of a pocket of his slacks and chose one from several. He did this, Bernie thought, as if it were a reflex.

"Don't bother to lock it, Mr. Meade," Bernie said. "Miss Curran and I will be here for a while yet."

"Of course," Meade said. "One gets into habits."

He went out of the door, leaving it open behind him. They could hear his footfalls on the tile floor of the corridor.

"We came to listen to a tape recording," Bernie said. "Still feel up to it, dear?"

Of course she felt up to it.

Which turned out not to matter, because the recorder, presumably with its tape in it, was not in either of the offices.

Bernie parked the green Chevrolet where it had been parked before, across the street from Nora's apartment house. He did not park it too close to a fire hydrant. And neither of them made any immediate move to get out of the car.

Bernie tried, as for so many hours he had been trying, to put things together in his mind. He found that he was going over some of them aloud.

"It could be," Bernie said, "that we know now why the key was returned, don't we? And who had a reason to return it."

She said, a little vaguely, "Do we, Bernie?"

"With Colley dead," Bernie said, "our little fidgeting professor could quit fidgeting about this book of his—this thing he had worked on for a good many years and been paid advances on. Advances Colley wanted back. Whether or not Meade had written what amounted to a letter of acceptance. The professor figuring rejection was Colley's personal decision, and that a dead man's decision doesn't hold. That with Colley dead the decision would be back to Meade."

"Yes, Bernie."

Her voice was faint, but its faintness did not reach into his mind.

"But," Bernie said, "murder might not—he might think it wouldn't—do any good if Meade himself got in bad trouble with the law. If, because he had the only key to the door between the offices, we might be able to prove that he had the only opportunity to murder. And Meade, if he knew, or guessed, that Colley's operation was one-man, and a very tentative one at that from the point of view of the board of directors and—where was I?"

"Something about a board of something," Nora said, in the same small, distant voice.

"Directors," Bernie said. "If Meade knew he had a good chance, with Colley dead, of staying on as editor. Of running the magazine which, if what he told Johnny Stein is true—if what Johnny guessed about it is true—is a major part of his life. Motive enough. Whole point of killing Colley is lost for the professor if Meade gets convicted of murder."

There was no answer. But Bernie, rambling in his own mind, did not listen for one.

"Another key in Meade's desk—a key anybody could have found and used—might seem to Armstrong to exonerate Meade. Not that Meade hasn't a pretty good alibi. But Armstrong probably doesn't know that. And come to think of it—"

Bernie stopped at that and sat silent for some minutes.

"We know Armstrong was around when Colley was killed," he said then. "That for a considerable time Meade's office wasn't locked. Time enough for Armstrong to get the key and, after Meade had left, use it. As somebody did, I think. Later, put it back for us to find. Thinking it would clear Meade of any suspicion. Not that it would, necessarily. But—provide a doubt. Reasonable doubt. Kill Colley. Go back through Meade's office and leave the key. Not in a place where it would be found immediately. In an out-of-the-way drawer corner where Meade might have put it years ago. But where it could be found by anyone with time enough and enough incentive. Only, I wonder, don't you dear, why—"

It occurred to him that he had not for some time heard any response, even a most dim reponse, from the girl on the seat beside him. He looked at her. He wished Stein could see how peaceful and how innocent Nora Curran looked when she was asleep.

He wakened her gently, and took her across the street. She was awake enough by then to find in her handbag the key which, at night, would let her into the apartment house, locked from midnight on. She found, too, the key to her own apartment and turned it in the lock while he waited.

"You're dead and no wonder," Bernie said. "Should I put you to bed?"

She wakened enough to smile up at him and to say, "I can make it, Bernie."

"Another time," Bernie said and kissed her gently. "And lock your door."

She went into the apartment and he could hear the lock click.

He walked the few blocks home, planning to do his wondering there. He went to sleep instead.

Waking and walking across a street and riding up in an elevator and hearing Bernie Simmons say "Another time" had broken sleep's first softness. Nora undressed and went to bed and waited for sleep's return. Its softness began, slowly, reluctantly, to creep around her and then somewhere there was a banging—a thudding sound which fragmented sleep.

Her room was on the street side and the window on the street was open. The sound seemed to come through the open window. She waited for it to stop, and when it did not stop got up and went to the window. She did not turn on light in the room. Faint light came through the window.

She looked down into an empty street—looked down at the tops of cars parked for the night on either side of it. At first nobody moved in the street. Then she looked toward the east, and almost at the next block, somebody was walking away from her.

A man or woman walking toward the east—or a shadow moving. Nothing which could be recognized—a moving shadow or a walking person, having, she thought, nothing to do with the thumpings she had heard, or thought that she had heard.

She went back to bed and almost instantly was asleep.

XIII

The telephone by his bed wakened Bernie Simmons and wakened him harshly. He lifted it and growled into it.

"Morning, Counselor," Lieutenant John Stein said to him. "Afraid I've got some news for you you won't like."

"At this hour," Bernie said, "any news is bad news, Johnny." He looked at his watch. It was a few minutes before nine o'clock. "Shoot."

"Miss Curran ran into something in the Chevy she rented," John Stein said. "With the right front fender, Counselor. Left a dent in it. It would have been a right front fender hit Fremont, Counselor."

"I know there's a dent in it," Bernie said. "And it's a very small dent, Johnny. Didn't crack the paint. At a guess, it could have happened—hell, months ago."

"The technical boys don't guess that way, Bernie," Stein said. "Went around early today, as soon as it was light, and it's not what they call a small dent. So they've towed it off to try their gimmicks on it. Offhand it's the kind of dent hitting somebody could cause. I think we'd better sort of talk about it, Bernie. About whether it isn't about time to bring a charge."

"All right," Simmons said. "Several things to talk to you about, Lieutenant. My office? In—oh, say about an hour?"

"I'll bring one of the tech boys along to tell you about the dent," Stein said. "About an hour."

"Have you got the tape recorder, Johnny?"

Stein had the tape recorder. Yes, he would bring it along to the office of the deputy chief of the District Attorney's Homicide Bureau if the deputy chief of the Homicide Bureau wanted him to. His voice indicated that he didn't see why anybody would want to listen to it again. His voice indicated, to Bernie Simmons, that the police already had all they needed to have.

"Johnny," Simmons said, "last night. Did you people search Meade's desk?"

"Went through it," Stein said. "Went through Colley's, too. We're very thorough people, Counselor."

"Looking for anything special?"

"Just checking things out."

"Find anything special?"

"Like a letter from somebody saying he'd just killed Colley? No, Bernie."

Stein was very patient.

"Like," Bernie said, "a key. A key which would fit the main door of Meade's office? And also the door between the offices?"

"No, Counselor. No kind of key at all."

"No," Bernie said. "I didn't think you would have, Lieutenant. About an hour, then."

Bernie was shaving, and waiting for coffee to drip through a Chemex, when the telephone rang again. He said, "Damn," which was suitable, and put the electric razor down and went to the telephone. He had not yet had coffee, so he growled into the telephone. A light, clear voice extinguished the growl.

"Bernie," Nora Curran said, "somebody's stolen my car."

Bernie hesitated. He didn't much like to say what he was going to have to say. He said it.

"No, dear," Bernie said. "The police towed it away."

"But this isn't a tow-away—" she said, and stopped and then said, "Oh."

"Yes," Bernie said, "I'm afraid that's it, Nora."

"But we—we looked. And it wasn't much of a dent, was it? Do they think—what do they think, Bernie? That they'll find blood on it?"

"No," Bernie said. "Threads of fabric, perhaps. Not blood. They won't, dear. But—"

He paused for a moment. He said, "How do you feel, darling? It was quite a night."

"I feel," Nora said, "that it was quite a night."

"Up," he said, "to coming down to my office in—oh, say an hour or so? As—call it corroborative testimony? As to what we found last night when we looked at the car? Because Johnny Stein isn't, just now, a very trusting man."

"Of course," she said. "Will the lieutenant arrest me, dear?"

The lightness in her voice was not especially convincing.

"The New York City police," Bernie told her, "do not bring homicide charges without the concurrence of the office of the District Attorney, County of New York. The office of the District Attorney of the County of New York does not concur. It's in Centre Street. Any taxi driver ought to know it. The Criminal Courts building."

She said, "Whatever you say, Bernie," and Bernie Simmons finished shaving and drank coffee. He even boiled himself an egg.

His office was on the seventh floor of the Criminal Courts building, and it was a small, hot office—hot even in the morning—and furnished with a desk and several wooden chairs. It was not air-conditioned. If Bernie ever got to be bureau chief instead of deputy chief he might get an air conditioner to go with rank.

Stein and a man Bernie did not know were waiting in the reception room Bernie walked through to get to the hallway which served his office. Stein's long dark face was not especially cheerful. He said, "Morning, Counselor," in a voice of no special cheer and picked up a carrying case which had a trade name stenciled on it and followed Bernie into the corridor and into the office. The man Bernie did not know followed them both.

"Sergeant Fleming," Stein said, when they were in the office. "Technical man. Tell the counselor about the fender, Fleming."

"At seven-fifteen this morning," Fleming said, "Patrolman Zensk and I proceeded to—"

"In English, if possible," Simmons said. "You're not in court, Sergeant. You went to look at a car and found a dent in the right front fender and called for a tow truck and had the car hauled off so you could make tests on it. So?"

"Evidence," the sergeant said, "that the car had run into something. Run into it hard. Deep dent in the right front fender. Chipped the paint."

"Any threads, or that sort of thing? From fabric we could identify?"

After the damaged fender had been photographed, paint samples at the apparent point of impact had been scraped off. The lab had them. The lab was running tests.

"All right," Bernie said. "Let's see the picture, Sergeant."

Sergeant Fleming got a photograph from a jacket pocket and handed it across Bernie Simmons's desk. It was a good clear photograph of a badly dented fender of an automobile. Bernie took it over to a window—to the only window—and looked at it in the light. He shook his head and sat down at the desk again and put the photograph on it.

"No, Johnny," Bernie said, "somebody's planted us a wrong tree to bark up. I had a look at the fender last night. Miss Curran and I both had a look at it. Dent, yes. But nothing like this."

He didn't think Stein was going to like that much.

"Miss Curran working for the Police Department now, Counselor?" Stein said. "And for that matter—" He didn't finish that. He did sigh.

"Come off it, Johnny," Bernie said. "We're on the same side."

"You and I and Miss Nora Curran," Stein said. "Who did run her car into something hard."

"Yes," Bernie said. "It looks that way, doesn't it?" He looked at the photograph again. Then he looked at Sergeant Fleming. "Something harder than a man, wouldn't you say, Sergeant?"

Sergeant Fleming said, "Well."

"You had a look at the car last night," Stein said. "Didn't find a dent. Not one like this. You and Miss Curran. Sure you looked at the right car, Counselor?"

"Miss Curran had a key to it," Bernie told him. "We used

it to drive over to *The Guardian* office after we'd looked at it. Using a flashlight, Johnny."

"Over to the *Guardian* office," Stein said. "Damn it to hell, Bernie. Oh, I know the way you are. God knows I've had plenty of chances to get used to it. But taking the girl—"

He shrugged his shoulders and spread his hands.

"She," Bernie said, "knows how to set up a tape recorder. Dictates into one herself."

"I'll bet she does," Stein said. "How to set one up and get it running."

"We didn't get that far," Simmons said. "Because you'd taken the recorder away with you."

"Paul Lane did," Stein said. "Comes to the same thing, of course. What did you expect to hear on the tape, Bernie? That we haven't all heard?"

"We tried opening and closing both doors," Bernie said. "And—"

He told Stein that one door's lock clicked audibly when the knob was turned and that the other did not. He said, "Let's play the start of it, Johnny."

Stein plugged the recorder in and flipped its switch.

For some seconds only surface sound from the tape came out of the amplifier. Then there was the click of a lock and, an instant afterward, the sound of a door closing. Then there was only the whir from the tape.

Stein said, "Hmmm."

"Yes," Bernie said. "When somebody turned the recorder on and went out of the office, wouldn't you—"

He stopped and they all listened. The surface sound went on and then a man said, "All right, Miss Pickett. Ask Mr. Simpson to come in." And a woman's voice said, "Yes, Mr. Colley."

"Damn formal, weren't they?" Stein said. "Considering—"

There was the sound of a door closing. Then there was a cough from the amplifier. There was a sound which might have been that of a desk drawer opening and closing. Then, this time for several minutes, there was only the tape's surface sound. That sound was interrupted only by Colley's voice.

Colley said, "Come in and sit down, Mr. Simpson. Mind closing the door?"

There was the sound of a door closing. Then, "We're going to make some changes in the magazine, Mr. Simpson. We're going to—"

"All right," Bernie said. "Mind turning it off, Johnny?"

Stein turned it off.

"Somebody turned the recorder on," Simmons said. "Walked across the office and turned a knob and the latch clicked. Went through, into Meade's office, wouldn't you say? —and closed the door after him. But—when Miss Pickett came in there wasn't any latch click, was there?"

"The door could have been open. The corridor door."

"Colley closed it after him when he came in," Simmons said. "Before he coughed. We heard it, Johnny."

"Proving?"

"Only suggesting," Bernie said, "that somebody turned the recorder on and went from Colley's office into Meade's. And that somebody came back through that door to kill Colley. Not through the door Miss Curran had just gone out of and closed after her."

"A lot to make out of clicks," Stein said. "But—maybe, Counselor. Somebody could have waited until Meade's office was empty and turned the recorder on and gone out that way. All right, so far. But when Meade left for the day he locked his office up. And locked the door between the two offices."

"Oh," Bernie said. "There was another key, Johnny."

He took the key out of his pocket and it rattled down on the desk.

"The one you didn't find," Bernie told the lieutenant of police. "Because, when you looked for it it wasn't there yet. Hadn't been put back. I think it was put back last night, after we left. After Paul Lane and the rest left."

Stein said he didn't get it. He said, "All right. Somebody found a key in Meade's desk and used it to go into the other office and kill Colley. And then put it back. Why put it back?"

"To get Meade off the hook. Partly off, anyway."

"Very considerate of somebody," Stein said. "Why the concern for Meade, Bernie?"

"With Meade still editor," Bernie said, "several people might stand to profit, Johnny. To the extent of their jobs. Or they may have thought so. Miss Curran and I weren't alone at the magazine offices last night, Johnny. Meade himself was there. So was our fidgety little professor."

He told Stein about Meade, who had been picking up a manuscript and looking for a key, and Armstrong, who had found a key and a letter. Stein said, "Hmmm."

"Armstrong had apparently been around for some time before we got there," Simmons said. "Would have had plenty of time to return the key. And, at a guess, reason enough to want to keep Meade off a hook."

He amplified that, briefly, as he had to Nora. When he thought of Nora, he looked at his watch. It had been considerably more than an hour since she had telephoned him and agreed to come to his office. Trouble getting a cab, he reassured himself.

"On the other hand," Bernie said, "any one of the possibles somebody set up for us could have come back earlier and dropped the key in Meade's desk. Anyone who had a key to what they call the back door. Simpson, Rosalie Shaffner, Miss Pickett, who says she's Mrs. Colley. Stubbs hasn't a key to the back door, Meade says. So we know where they were last night?"

"Those," Stein said. "And Miss Curran, Bernie. You sort of keep leaving her out. Where was she?"

Bernie told him where Nora Curran had gone in her rented green Chevrolet.

"Check it out?"

"No."

"Anybody else you would have," Stein said. "So we will, Bernie. Got a telephone book?"

Simmons did have. "Werkes, Isadore, M.D." was listed twice in the Manhattan directory. The telephone was answered at the number listed as "Res." After a brief time, Dr. Werkes came on. Stein identified himself. He understood that one of the doctor's patients, a Miss Dorothy Curran, had, for a time at any rate, been missing during the night from the doctor's sanitarium in Westchester.

"I don't," Dr. Werkes said, "know where you got that understanding. Or that it is any concern of yours. I don't discuss my patients with outsiders. No matter who they profess to be on the telephone."

"It may be important," Stein said. "Did Dorothy Curran turn up missing last night? Even for a brief time? And did somebody there telephone her sister?"

"I don't give out information about my patients," Werkes said.

"You have a patient named Dorothy Curran?"

"Yes."

"And you are treating her in the sanitarium?"

Stein was holding the receiver a little way from his ear, so that Bernie Simmons could hear the answers. The answer to the last question was, "I have said all I intend to about my patients, Lieutenant. If you are a lieutenant." That was followed by the crack of a replaced telephone.

"Cagey," Bernie said. "Doctors get that way. If the girl hadn't been missing for a time last night, he'd have had no special reason to be cagey, I'd think. But I suppose you'll have a man make a little trip up to Westchester."

"Yes," Stein said. "Oh, yes, Counselor. As for the others—"

As for Rosalie Shaffner, friends had lent her a house, and a car to go with it, a short distance north of New Canaan. She had been in the house—had, at any rate, been lying on a chaise on the terrace of the house—an hour or so ago. She had been drinking breakfast coffee.

As for Adele Colley, née Pickett, she had not left the apartment house she lived in, at least by the front door, during the night. There had been a man across the street, watching. She had not taken her car out of the garage in the basement of the building in West Fifty-seventh Street, according to the night man on duty there.

As for H. R.—for Hezekiah Rudolph—Stubbs, his car

had been parked in his driveway at around eleven and for several hours thereafter, when the state trooper had stopped touring past the house.

"None of it's very tight, is it?" Simmons said. "We know Dr. Armstrong was there."

"And your girl was," Stein said. "And could have been earlier. And that, come to that, Meade was himself. You say Miss Curran was the one who found the key in Meade's desk?"

"Yes."

"Seem to have much trouble finding it, Bernie?"

"Had to look through several drawers," Simmons said. "Found it in the last one."

"And picked it up? The way one picks a key up normally, holding it flat? And, what? Gave it to you?"

"Yes. And I held it the same way, Lieutenant. So there won't be any nice clean prints."

"Sort of rubbed the key between your fingers?"

"Not consciously," Bernie said. "I may have."

"Pity, Counselor," Stein said. "Really a pity. I'd have expected better from an experienced man like you. Can't be helped now. But—I'll take the key, Counselor. Our tech boys are pretty good, sometimes."

Simmons didn't answer that, except to flick the key across the desk with his right index finger. He picked up his telephone and got an outside line and dialed a number. Stein could hear the signal which meant a telephone bell was ringing somewhere. Simmons let it ring a good many times before he put the receiver back in its cradle.

"She's a hard one to get on the telephone, isn't she?" Stein said.

Bernie did not answer that, either. He looked at his watch. An hour and a half, now, since she had called. Of course, she may have had to dress and make breakfast. Of course she may have had to walk blocks before she found a taxi.

"Could be," Stein said, "she's thought of some place she'd rather be."

"She's on her way here," Bernie said. "To tell you what we saw when we looked at the car fender together. Since you don't seem very trusting, Johnny. And—if anything waked her up after I left her last night—this morning. And—"

He stopped suddenly and looked at the wall behind John Stein. He looked at it fixedly, but not as if he were looking at a wall.

"And," he said, and spoke slowly to the wall, "if Meade offered her a drink last night when he sent his car to take her to his house. And—whether he had a drink himself."

Simmons picked up the photograph of the damaged car fender and took it back to the window and looked at it again. He said, "Sergeant. Come here a minute where the light's—"

The telephone rang on Bernie's desk and he was only a long stride from it.

"Ask Miss Curran to come in," he said, and put the telephone back.

He had, of course, been a fool to worry because a girl was a few minutes late. Tenderness can do odd things to a man when it comes on him suddenly, in an active sort of way.

XIV

The female of the species is, at any rate, more resilient than the male, Bernie Simmons thought when Nora came into the little, hot office. Bernie himself was missing sleep, and was pretty certain he showed it. Nora, on the other hand, was crisp from glossy brown hair to white summer shoes. She wore a yellow dress, belted with darker yellow. She looked fine.

"I'm late," she said. "I had to wait—" She spoke to Bernie and stopped speaking when she saw Lieutenant Stein. She said, in another voice, "Oh, good morning, Lieutenant." Then she looked at Bernie and her eyes widened.

She turned back to Stein. "Mr. Simmons," she said, "says you're not a trusting man, Lieutenant."

"Well," Stein said, "I'm not exactly paid to be, Miss Curran. There's a point about this car of yours that—"

"The fender we looked at, Nora," Bernie said. "Seems the police found a good deal more damage than you and I did."

He was still at the window, still holding the photograph. Sergeant Fleming, who had started to join him there, had stopped when the telephone rang.

"They've got a picture of it," Bernie said. "Come over here by the light, Nora."

She went over to the window and they both looked at the photograph. She turned back and looked at Stein.

"Probably you won't believe me," she said, "but it wasn't anything like that. It was—you could hardly see it was dented."

"So Mr. Simmons says," Stein told her. "Could be, of course, somebody—oh, backed into it after you and Mr.

Simmons had parked it. After you'd gone over the office and found this second key. And, of course, after you had taken this trip to the country about your sister."

"Which," Nora said, "you don't believe either, do you? So you called Dr. Werkes to check on me. And he wasn't forthcoming, was he? He's like that. Good doctors don't talk about their patients."

"What makes you think I checked with the doctor, Miss Curran?"

"The doctor," she said. "He called me up. One of the things that made me late here, Bernie. That and no taxicabs. He hadn't known that—that my sister was missing for a while last night. They'd tried to reach him, but he'd been out. After you talked to him he called his place up in the country and they told him about it. And he called me just as I was about to leave the apartment. And, Lieutenant, they told him that they'd called me."

"Clears that up," Stein said. "According to what Mr. Simmons says, you went only part way up and telephoned and found out everything was all right and came back to town."

"Yes," Nora said. "And they told the doctor about my calling, Lieutenant. And they'll tell you."

Stein said he was sure they would. He said, "The car was parked almost directly across from your apartment house, Miss Curran. Your bedroom on the front of the building? Because, if somebody backed into the Chevy after you and Mr. Simmons re-parked it, there'd have been quite a racket. Judging by the damage done. Hear anything like that—a crashing sound? Rending metal?"

"No, nothing like that. But there was—or I dreamed there was—" She stopped for a moment.

"My window was open," she said. "It's over the street, yes, And—some time, I don't know precisely when, but I'd dropped off to sleep—there was a noise from the street. A kind of dull pounding noise. It's—now it's hazy. I may have dreamed it— and dreamed that I went to the window and looked down. And the street was empty."

"Nobody on it?" Bernie asked her.

"Empty," she said, but then, "wait. Down at the end of the block I thought I saw somebody. Walking away."

"Somebody? Man or woman?"

"Just a figure. Indistinct. Maybe, of course, I dreamed that, too."

"No," Bernie said, "I don't think you dreamed it, dear. And—Johnny, suppose you take a good hard look at this photograph."

Stein said, "O.K., Counselor," and took the photograph. He looked at it for some seconds, turning it this way and that way in his hands. Then he said, "Hmmm," and gave it back.

"Nora," Bernie said, "when you went over to Mr. Meade's house last night. To be told you had a new and better job. Meade offer you a drink to celebrate with?"

"Yes."

"Take it?"

"Yes. He expected me to."

"Have one himself?"

"His man—chauffeur or houseman or whatever—brought us both drinks."

"What did you have, Nora?"

"A Scotch and water."

"And Mr. Meade?"

"Something in a tall glass," she said. "A—a kind of blurry drink. Wait—"

Bernie waited.

"What he had last night," she said. "This morning, really. A—didn't he say it was a Scotch mist, Bernie?"

"Yes," Bernie Simmons said. "A Scotch mist, dear. Very cooling drink in hot water. Ever try one, Johnny?"

"Mostly," John Stein said, "I drink beer. Otherwise, bourbon. Mind if I ask Miss Curran something, Counselor?"

He put a good deal of inflection into the question. He was a junior asking permission. Bernie laughed at him and Stein, after an instant of keeping a straight face, grinned back.

"Had you any idea, Miss Curran," Stein asked her, "that if Mr. Simpson left the magazine for some reason—for any reason—you would get his job? Any idea at all?"

"None. Or that Kent ever thought of leaving. We'd—oh, we'd been going over things that would have carried us for many months ahead."

"At all as if he were laying things out for you? Giving you sort of a running start?"

"No. Anyway, that never entered my mind. We always plan a good way ahead. Have to. Particularly on the one-shots."

Stein shrugged his shoulders and raised his eyebrows.

"Novels complete in one issue," she said. "They're not, really. Condensed novels. We're four or five months ahead on them, usually."

Stein said he saw. He looked at Bernie Simmons and raised his eyebrows again.

Then he said, "Could be you've got something, Bernie. Maybe we ought to go and ask."

"Yes," Bernie said. "Maybe we'd better, Johnny. And take Miss Curran with us, wouldn't you think?"

"I don't—" Stein said, and stopped and nodded his head.

"Might be an idea," he said. "It might very well, Bernie."

"In an hour or so," Bernie said. "Get there after the sun's over the yardarm. Could be he'll offer us a drink."

They went to a restaurant and killed time over coffee. At about noon they drove uptown in the police sedan, which was not identified as a police sedan. Jefferson Meade's Cadillac was parked in front of Meade's narrow house. There was just room behind it for Fleming to park the car. There was somewhat more space in front. "Park in front, Fleming," Stein said and Fleming parked the sedan in front of the big Cadillac. "We may be a while," Stein said. "Just sit tight, Sergeant."

Fleming said, "Sir." The New York Police Department is a quasi-military organization.

"Remember to look worried, Nora," Bernie Simmons said, as they went up the three white steps to the door of Meade's house.

"That," Nora said, "will be the easiest thing possible, Bernie."

Stein rang the doorbell and almost at once the door opened. Meade himself opened it.

He said, "Lieutenant. Mr. Simmons," and then, after an instant's break, "Oh, Miss Curran." Then he said, "Do come in," and held the door open for them.

"A point or two," Stein said. "Sorry to bother you again."

It wasn't any bother, Meade told them, and led them into the living room they had been in before. He walked erect, his shoulders square under a blue polo shirt, his hips slim under dark slacks. Inside the long, narrow room he said, "Sit down, won't you?" He looked at his watch. He said, "Can I offer you drinks? Miss Curran?"

"I don't—" she said. She looked anxiously at Simmons, at Stein.

"No reason why not, Miss Curran," Bernie said. He clipped the words; chipped them at her.

"A very mild Scotch and plain water," Nora said, and Meade nodded his head and looked at Bernie Simmons.

"Whatever you're having, Mr. Meade," Bernie said. "Anything that's handy. Scotch would be fine."

"This kind of weather," Meade said, "I go in for long drinks. Gin and tonic?"

"I don't drink gin much," Bernie said, with considerable disregard for the truth. "But, if that's handiest."

"All handy," Meade said. "Myself, I'm having a Scoth mist. Favorite of mine in the summer."

Bernie told him that that would be fine. Stein said, "I don't often drink at noon, Mr. Meade. But a touch of bourbon on the rocks. Just a spot, if you don't mind."

"Spot it is," Meade said. He reached out toward the table near the chair he had chosen and pulled his hand back.

"Forgot for a moment," he said. "Alfred's off today. Fact is, I'm planning to drive up to the country for the rest of the weekend."

He stood up and walked down the long narrow room and went through a door at the end of it.

"Worried enough?" Nora said, her voice low.

"Doing fine, darling," Simmons said.

He got up and walked down the room and stopped near the door at the end of it. He stood there a few minutes and then, rather quickly, turned toward the nearest wall and began to look at the books in shelves against it. Meade came through the door, which apparently led to the kitchen area. He was carrying a tray with filled glasses on it. After he had passed Bernie, and as Bernie turned to follow him back up the room, Bernie briefly shook his head. Stein, who was looking at him, made no response.

Meade put glasses down on tables beside chairs and carried one of the Scotch mists back to his own chair. He said, "Cheers," and the men lifted their glasses without saying anything. Nora lifted hers just from the table, and it seemed to shake in her hand and she put it down again.

"Before your point or two, Lieutenant," Meade said. "I've got one of my own. Part of one, anyway. I told you I almost remembered the license number of the car that hit poor Fremont?"

"Yes. Three N, you thought. Couldn't remember the rest. Come back to you, Mr. Meade?"

"Not all of it," Meade said. "Three N I'm sure of. And then, I'm pretty sure, the digits five and eight. Maybe a zero then. But it may have been a nine. Help any?"

Stein took a pad from his pocket. It had a pencil clipped to it. He wrote on the pad. He said, "Narrows it down, Mr. Meade." He put the pad back in his pocket.

"My—" Nora said and stopped.

Bernie Simmons said, "Yes, Miss Curran?" He spoke very quickly.

"Nothing," Nora said. "Oh, I think the license number of the car I'm renting begins with three N."

She lifted her glass again, and her hand shook.

"Remember the rest of it?" Stein said.

She shook her head.

"One of the points," Stein said. "Reason we asked Miss Curran to come along, actually. She tells us you told her that Simpson's decision not to come back to *The Guardian* was a complete surprise to you. Just want to confirm that."

Meade looked thoughtfully at his glass and for some seconds said nothing. Then he said, "Did I really give you that impression, Miss Curran? That I was surprised at Kent Simpson's decision?"

"Yes," Nora said. "I was sure it was a surprise to you. As much as it was to me."

"Well," Meade said, and drew the word out. "So, it was to you, Miss Curran? I'd thought—no matter. No, Lieutenant, it wasn't a complete surprise to me. Simpson never put it in so many words, but I'd begun to feel in the last several months that he was turning the job over in his mind. Whether to keep it, I mean. Or go back to free-lance writing. He did mention he was working on a book. He said something like, 'With what's left of me after I finish here.' Something like that."

Meade stopped to light a cigarette. Then he said, "Sorry," and made a motion with the cigarette box, reaching it out toward Nora Curran. She said, "Thank you, Mr. Meade," and got a cigarette out of the box. She had a little trouble in getting it out, because her fingers seemed unsteady.

"Nothing definite," Meade said. "I mean about his quitting. About you, Miss Curran, he was most definite. Had a high regard for your work. One time—I remember this now—he said something about your being able to take over his job any time. That you had a real feel for, understanding of, our readers. That you, a lot more than he, were in the right age group to have—what did he say? Of course, empathy with them. 'If I'm not around,' he said—something like that—'you couldn't do better than Miss Curran.'"

"I didn't know he felt that way," Nora said. "Oh, that we worked well together. That he was satisfied with me as an assistant."

"Funny," Meade said. "I got the impression he'd—"

He stopped and shook his head.

"That he'd what, Mr. Meade?" Bernie asked the tall lean man, who was turning his glass slowly between his fingers.

"All right," Meade said. "That he'd talked over with Miss Curran the possibility of her taking his place on the staff. Seems I was wrong."

Bernie said, "Well, Miss Curran?" He spoke sharply and turned in his chair to face her.

Her face twitched for an instant. Then she said, "No, Mr. Simmons. There was never anything like that I remember. Or anything about the possibility of his quitting."

Bernie looked at John Stein. Stein shook his head, slowly.

"It's true," Nora said, and her voice went up a little. "I tell you it's *true.*"

She lifted her drink and again it shook a little in her hand.

"Why don't you ask me straight out?" she said, and now her voice was almost shrill. "I didn't know I'd get Mr. Simpson's job if he quit. I didn't know that Mr. Colley was—was so important. That his death would make the difference Mr. Meade says it does."

"All right, Miss Curran," Bernie said and finished his drink. He also blinked his eyelids at her. He was still turned to face her and turned away from Meade. He turned back to Meade, who was looking thoughtfully at Nora Curran. He moved his head slowly from side to side as he looked at her.

Bernie finished his drink, draining whisky from crushed ice. He said, "You're right, Mr. Meade. It's a good drink in hot weather."

"Get you another," Meade said, and started to stand up.

"Trouble to make," Bernie said. "Ice cubes to crush and everything. I could do with another but just on the rocks will be fine. No use all that pounding up of cubes."

"I don't," Meade said. "I just drop them in a gadget and push a button." He stood up and reached out for Bernie's glass.

"Go along with you and lend a hand," Bernie Simmons said. "Like to see this gadget of yours. Me, I'm primitive. When I want to crush ice I use a canvas bag and a mallet."

"Alfred used to do that," Meade said. "Then he saw an advertisement of this electric crusher—Hammacher Schlemmer, as I remember it—and suggested we buy one. By all means, come along and have a look at it, Mr. Simmons."

The two tall men walked the length of the room together and went through the door at the end of it. Each of them carried a tall glass, and in the bottom of each glass crushed ice, faintly colored by Scotch whisky, sloshed a little.

"Odd," Nora said to Stein, who was looking at her with the smallest of possible smiles. "I never knew Bernie was so fond of Scotch. A martini man, I'd always thought."

"Circumstances alter tastes, maybe," Stein said. "Do you really happen to remember the license number of this car of yours, Miss Curran?"

"Yes, I looked it up for Bernie," she said. "Gave it to him."

"And it starts the way Mr. Meade—" Stein began, and stopped abruptly.

Meade came through the door at the end of the room, carrying his glass, full now with crushed ice and Scotch. He was alone.

"Be right along," Meade said, when he was half way up the long room. "Stopped a minute in the—"

He did not finish. He carried his glass to his table and sat in his chair. He said, "The other points, Lieutenant?"

"We'll wait for Mr. Simmons," Stein said. "Although I think we've covered most of them."

Meade looked at Stein's almost full glass. He said, "You're not drinking, Lieutenant."

"Almost never do in the middle of the day," Stein said. "Particularly when I'm on duty, Mr. Meade."

"I realize I shouldn't ask," Meade said. "But in a sense I'm involved, of course. My shop and that sort of thing. Are you and Mr. Simmons making progress?"

"We may be," Stein said. "We may—"

He broke off and looked across at Nora Curran. He looked hard at her.

"We very well may be," he said. "This business about Mr. Simpson may—"

He stopped. Bernie Simmons came through the door at the end of the room. He was not carrying a glass. He was carrying a wooden mallet. He was carrying it with a paper towel wrapped around the handle.

It was a dark mallet with a squared-off head. Simmons

carried it as if it were a rather heavy mallet. He put it down on a table beside John Stein.

"Mahogany," Simmons said. "Not just the common kitchen variety. Rather an elegant item, Johnny. Metal handle with engraving on it. But the head is scarred up a bit, isn't it? As if it had been pounded on something harder than ice, wouldn't you say?"

Stein looked at the mallet. He pulled the paper towel off, without touching the engraved metal handle.

"Yes," he said, "does seem to be banged up a bit."

"As if," Bernie Simmons said, "somebody had banged it against metal, wouldn't you say?"

"You could say that," Stein said.

He put the paper back around the handle and picked the mallet up and examined the head slowly, with care.

"Been washed," he said. "But the technical boys are pretty good with their gadgets. Break paint with wood and flakes of paint are likely to get embedded."

Meade leaned forward in his chair and looked at them while they examined the mallet. And then Bernie looked at him.

"Trouble is, Mr. Meade," Bernie said, "you edited too much. Should have left it nice and blurry, the way you started it when you turned the recorder on. Left it to us to pick and choose. When did you decide to make it Miss Curran, Meade? Instead of just leaving it open?"

Meade said what Bernie expected him to say. He said, "I haven't the faintest idea what you're talking about."

But he put a hand on each arm of the chair, as if he were about to come out of it. And Stein leaned forward in his chair.

"Gave us six to start with," Simmons said. "When you turned on the recorder to run while Colley fired people—fired them rudely, abruptly. Figured, rightly, that we'd run the tape. Listen to Simpson and Fremont and Stubbs and Armstrong and Miss Shaffner and Miss Curran. All getting fired. Six to choose from Meade. Why narrow it down? Edit it down to Miss Curran?"

"You're not making any sense," Meade said.

Bernie Simmons did not seem to hear him.

"Just now," Simmons said, "by trying to convince us that Miss Curran knew she would get Simpson's job if he gave it up. And, early this morning, by banging up her car with the mallet—this mallet, Meade—you used at the office this morning to break ice with and carried away with you when you left. After Miss Curran and I had left. You slipped up there, Meade. Should have thrown the mallet away as soon as you'd used it on the car. Shouldn't have it at all, come to that. Dents, impressions, the mallet made will match up. Not at all the kind of damage which would be done to a car by hitting a man. You should have thought of that. Look at the right front fender of your own car, Meade. We did. No dent at all. But that's what hit Fremont and threw him across the sidewalk head first into the steps of a house up the street."

Meade did not say anything. But he edged foward in his chair, tensed in his chair.

"Why Miss Curran?" Bernie said again. "Because you were afraid she'd seen you when you went back to the office last night? Dressed in different clothes. Looking like a tourist in the city? Wanted to persuade us that anything she said about that would be said only to protect herself?"

He turned to Nora Curran.

"By the way," he said, "you don't remember seeing him, Nora?"

"No. I—I wasn't seeing much of anything right then, Bernie."

"Fremont did see you, didn't he, Meade? Reason he came here last night, wasn't it? To give you a chance to explain? Was that it? Or—to shake you down?"

Meade came up out of his chair, the heavy highball glass in his hand. He threw the glass at Bernie Simmons. Bernie's hands flew up to ward it off, but they were not quick enough. The base of the glass hit him on the forehead and the contents of the glass flew out and down his face and into his eyes.

Meade ran then. He ran toward the door to the entrance hall. He did not make it. He ran into John Stein before he reached the door.

XV

It was still hot in New York on Monday night. In Nora's apartment the living room was only faintly cooled by the window air conditioner. He made them martinis—martinis for the road before they went out to dinner. They raised their glasses to each other and Bernie said, "You look fine tonight, darling. The finest of all possible girls."

She wore a black summer sheer and she looked fine. Bernie felt tenderness flowing out toward her. Of course it was tenderness. Active tenderness. She said, "Thank you, Bernie."

He said, "How did things go at the office?"

"Confusingly," she said. "Nobody worked much. Oh, Nelson Barclay is coming back. He'll take over, apparently, until—until things are settled. If they're ever settled."

"You?"

"Kent Simpson's coming back, too. Since there's an emergency. For not more than a couple of weeks, he says. To tide over. The rest I don't know about. Nobody really knows about the rest."

She sipped from her glass. She said, "All right, Bernie. Give. You've got a bump on your head."

Bernie said he knew he had a bump on his head.

"Meade isn't being helpful," Bernie said. "Standing on his rights. Calling in a lawyer, which is the brightest thing he's done yet. Oh, the technical boys did find paint splinters in the mallet head. Match the paint on the Chevy. Which will help."

They would, he said, need help. "It's one thing to reconstruct," Bernie said. "It's another thing to persuade a jury."

"You will? You and Lieutenant Stein? By the way, he's convinced now I wasn't the one?"

Quite convinced, Bernie told her. And yes, he thought they would get what they needed to persuade a jury. Now that they knew what they had to have.

"He turned on the tape recorder to provide suspects," Nora said. "Then he went home. There'll be any number of people to say they saw him leave, won't there?"

That wasn't the trouble, Bernie said. Those people they had. The trouble was to find somebody who had seen Jefferson Meade coming back.

"All right," Nora said, "reconstruct, Bernie."

Meade had found out that Colley's plans for *The Guardian* were solely Colley's plans, agreed to by the network's board doubtfully; subject to reconsideration if Colley wasn't around. "He found out from a member of the board," Bernie said. "Paul Lane has already found the member. Says, sure Meade knew there was a lot of opposition to the changes Colley wanted in the magazine."

Meade had planned ahead. Hence the tape recorder. He had left the party when he said he did. He had walked home. Or, possibly, got a cab home. He had made certain that his man, Alfred, saw him come home and knew what time it was when he did come. He had told Alfred to pick up the car. He had changed from his gray suit—the gray suit he always wore—into dark slacks and dark polo shirt.

"Midsummer in New York," Bernie said, "the place is full of tourists. Wear a lot of sports clothes, tourists do. Natives don't look at them twice, unless the men wear funny shirts."

Meade had turned on the shower, for Alfred's benefit, not his own. "It gurgles." He had seen Alfred go out to get the car. He had gone out himself and walked back to the office and, going from his own office into Colley's, killed Colley. And turned off the recorder, probably before he killed. The party was over, then. He had, presumably, used the back door both when he came in and when he went out.

"So far we haven't found anybody who saw him come or go," Bernie said. "We will, unless he was very lucky. Come and go in the office, I mean. Fremont saw him in the lobby downstairs. Which was too bad for Fremont."

"Fremont tried to blackmail him? And Meade ran him down with the Cadillac. And made up the green Chevrolet?"

"One at a time, darling," Bernie said. "I'm not sure that Fremont tried to shake him down. Not in character, if Fremont was at all the kind of man his sister thinks he was. More likely, give Meade a chance to explain how he happened to go back to the office building in a polo shirt and dark slacks. Ran him down in the Caddy. Yes. Because he hasn't been able to convince the little clergyman that everything was on the up and up."

As for the green Chevrolet—

That was, Bernie thought, something that grew on Meade as he thought about it. "Edited it. Shaped it to fit you, Nora." At first, he hadn't been sure of the make of the killing car, or of its color. Or of the complete license number.

"Got the rest of the number of your car while he was banging it up," Bernie said. "Decided to remember it gradually. When he thought remembering it would do him the most good."

After killing Colley, Meade had gone home. Probably he had walked. It was only a few blocks and walking would have been the quickest way across town. As Meade had expected, Alfred hadn't yet returned with the car. Meade had changed to dinner clothes and gone to his party.

"All worked pretty much as he'd planned it," Bernie said. "Trouble for him was that he went on planning. They do, a lot of the time. Try to patch up things which don't really need patching."

The second key was, of course, one of the things that did need patching up. Meade had been right to have second thoughts about that. With only one key, and that in Meade's pocket, Meade would be the only person who could get from one office to the other.

"Had the duplicate key in the desk in his house, probably," Bernie said. "Took it over and put it in the office desk. Got there before we did, which was a break for him. He had a good many breaks, until he tried to make his own. But murder's always a chancy business."

"Why? He wasn't being fired."

Actually, Bernie told her, it came pretty much to that. At any rate, he was going to be retired; retired a year before he reached the compulsory age. Paul Lane had found that out, too, from the board member he had talked to.

"Bits and pieces," Bernie said. "When we know what bits and pieces we're looking for. But—I'm guessing about this, and we won't have to prove anything about it—I doubt if it was merely that he was being pushed out. I think he killed to save a magazine. A magazine he'd devoted most of his life to. A magazine which had pretty much become his life. I suspect that, to him, the changes Colley planned were—well, sacrilege."

"But to kill a man."

"Values get distorted," Bernie said. "Always, in a murderer's mind, they are distorted, Nora. Otherwise there wouldn't be murder. Murder is a distortion, dear."

He looked at her; saw questions move across her delicate face as she mulled over the things he had said. Probably "Murder is a distortion" didn't make any real sense to her. Bernie wasn't sure it did to him, either.

"Another before we go?" Bernie said, after a long pause. "It's pleasant here."

She smiled at him and there was, he thought, a kind of tenderness in the way she smiled. Of course "tenderness" was the word for it.

"It is, isn't it?" Nora Curran said. "And quiet. Perhaps we might have one more before we go out to dinner, dear."

SOUTH ORANGE PUBLIC LIBRARY

3 9507 00037565 8

WITHDRAWN

M
Lockridge, Richard
A plate of red herrings.

JAN 26 1998

DEC 26 1998

7-69